Ellen Anders on Her Own

Ellen Anders on Her Own

KAREN HIRSCH

MACMILLAN PUBLISHING COMPANY
New York

Maxwell Macmillan Canada
Toronto

Maxwell Macmillan International
New York   Oxford   Singapore   Sydney

J / H

First edition. Printed in the United States of America
10 9 8 7 6 5 4 3 2 1
The text of this book is set in 12.5 point Berkeley Oldstyle Book.

Library of Congress Cataloging-in-Publication Data
Hirsch, Karen.   Ellen Anders on her own / by Karen Hirsch. — 1st ed.   p.   cm.
Summary: Eleven-year-old Ellen gains insight into her changing friendships after reading her deceased mother's girlhood diary.   ISBN 0-02-743975-5
[1. Friendship — Fiction. 2. Schools — Fiction. 3. Diaries — Fiction. 4. Death — Fiction.] I. Title.   PZ7.H59788E1   1994   [Fic] — dc20   93-13350

For Stephanie, David, and Tim

1

On a spring day, six months after her mom's death, Ellen Anders sat in the noisy sixth-grade room surrounded by kids she had known since preschool. Her chin in one propped-up hand, she listened to Mr. Fitzgerald talk about poetry. He had written *senses* on the board in big, pink chalk letters.

"Remember the afternoon we spent outside, sensing nature and writing poetry?" he asked, twirling the chalk in his hand. He rested his tall, lean body against the heavy wooden desk at the front of the room.

"Yeah, I wrote a good one about a worm, Mr. Fitz," blurted Sam Sturtz.

Ellen smiled at Sam's outburst and thought about that poetry-writing day a few weeks ago. She twirled a hank of her long, fine blond hair around her finger and remembered the warm sun on the patch of moss where she had sat in the woods by the school, writing and feeling, for once, free of her constant thoughts of her mom.

Mr. Fitz grinned at Sam and the rest of the class as he tucked the long piece of chalk behind his ear. He went on. "Well, today I'd like you to choose one poem from that day to polish for a Mother's Day card," he said.

"Choose one with sensory detail and let your mom be in the field or those woods with you. Let her see what you saw. Let her touch what you touched." Mr. Fitz waved his long arms, picking imaginary flowers, smoothing grass, and holding up a rock or a bug. "Let her smell what you smelled!"

A Mother's Day card! Ellen shivered and creased her dark, thick eyebrows over her closed eyes. She heard her classmates chatter as they settled down to work.

"Oh, yuck, I'd rather buy one!"

"Great! I'll use my tree roots one."

"I'm going to choose my green bug poem."

"I hate poetry."

"I love poetry."

Ellen let the hubbub, so typical in Mr. Fitz's classroom, cover for her as she paged through her writing folder, pretending to search for a poem. She slumped like a rag doll against the hard back of her seat and remembered the day, last November, that her dad had come to school to tell her about the car accident and her mom's death.

Ellen could hardly remember the first day—just the crying, and Grandma and Grandpa, Mom's parents, arriving, and then the minister coming, and her dad holding her as if she were a first grader. The memorial service had been on a school day, and Mr. Fitz and Mrs. Johanson, the principal, had both been there. About ten kids from her class had come, too.

Back at school the next week, everyone had treated

her the way her mom had treated the antique Hummel figurine, "Weary Wanderer," that sat on the mantel at home, as if she might break, or break down, at any moment. They had been very quiet and very nice to her, for a while. Even Olivia Von Cracken and the other Dandy Dames had quit teasing her about being a nerd. But gradually nearly everyone had seemed to forget, and things had gotten back to normal. For everyone but Ellen, that is.

Ellen came back to the present and stared at her sheet of paper. How could Mr. Fitz make me do this, she thought while her classmates worked happily around her.

"I can't think of a rhyme for *buttercup*," called Kyle Bloss, the boy who sat across the aisle.

"Poems don't have to rhyme, stupid," said Cassie Conrath, who sat in front of him.

Students milled around, sharing scissors and stopping to read one another's poems. Ellen sat, limp and weak, until finally her classmates settled down with their construction and tissue paper, glue, scissors, and writing folders. Ellen saw her two best friends, Abby Wickers and Jen Coleman, go up to Mr. Fitz. She watched him as they talked.

Then he walked over to her. "Ellen, this is hard for you," he said, pulling up a student chair near her desk.

"Not hard, Mr. Fitz," Ellen said quietly. "Impossible." She ducked her head, angry at Mr. Fitz and at the tears that had come.

"Could you make one for your grandma?" Mr. Fitz asked. "Or your aunt?"

"They're not my mother, Mr. Fitz," Ellen said, and she lay her head down on her arm to hide the tears. "I don't want to talk," she said.

Mr. Fitz put his hand on her shoulder. "I'm sorry, Ellen," he said. "I hope that Mother's Day will be a day of good memories for you." He moved away, and as Ellen slipped out of her desk to go to the bathroom, she saw the dark, sober look on his long face.

She washed her face in the sink and rinsed it again and again in cold water. Then she rubbed her skin with brown paper towels until her face was red and smelled of cardboard. She went into a stall and pulled off some toilet paper to blow her nose. Finally she walked slowly back to her classroom.

Even with her eyes pointed toward the worn wooden floorboards, Ellen felt the stares of her classmates as she walked across the back of the room. She knew her still-streaked face was getting redder as she tried to move quickly up the aisle toward her desk. Suddenly her shoe caught on the edge of an open three-ring binder on the floor by Olivia's desk. She slid forward, tottered, then grabbed the nearest desk to balance herself. It was only her slender, lithe body and quick reflexes that saved her from falling flat on her face. She heard Olivia's muffled burst of laughter.

Ellen turned her head away, bit her lip to keep from crying more, and hurried to her own desk. She sat down and flipped with pretended interest through her writing folder. Looking up, she saw Abby make a detour on her way to the art table to walk by her desk. Carefully, Ellen opened the little note Abby had left. It was written on a sheet of notepaper decorated with a cartoon penguin and the words *From the desk of Abby* at the top. Remembering Mr. Fitz's No-note-passing rule, Ellen hid the note behind her writing folder.

Mr. Fitz had a high tolerance for other things, he'd often said, but note passing wasn't one of them. According to him, they'd rue the day they passed a note and got caught. If they liked being embarrassed, just pass notes, he'd told the class.

Early in September, Mr. Fitz had read two notes aloud to the class and had posted them on the bulletin board for all but the writers to laugh about. "Dear Jodi," one note had said, "I think Cindra's the most stuck-up kid in the room. Don't you? Write back. From Anna."

Since that humiliating day, people in Mr. Fitz's class passed notes rarely and with exceeding caution. Now Ellen made sure Mr. Fitz was busy before she casually opened her folder and unfolded the note.

The note said, "Maybe your mom can still know that you love her. Somehow, maybe. From your best friend, Abby." Abby had drawn a smiley face at the bottom of the sheet, and Ellen couldn't help but look across at Abby and smile a little at her.

Jen, who sat behind Ellen, leaned forward. "Your trillium poem was good. You could use that one," she said.

Ellen turned around. Whispering in Mr. Fitz's class was no problem, ever—except at test time. Ellen didn't try to hide her teary face as she looked at Jen, who sat with papers, markers, and glue spread across her desk. "Oh, Jen," she said, "I can't do this."

Jen reached over and touched Ellen's shoulder. She tilted her head to one side and made a funny face as she always did when Ellen needed cheering up. Ellen felt soothed by the sight of her friend's freckly face and long, dark curly hair. "Well, maybe I'll try it," she said. "Thanks, Jen."

Ellen got up slowly and walked toward the supply table. She went the long way to avoid Olivia. Stopping at the Reading Cove, she slumped into the old gold-and-green plaid sofa Mr. Fitz had put there. She looked around the classroom at all the others busily writing and drawing cards for their mothers. Suddenly she noticed Abby stop at Olivia's desk and saw them laugh together. Ellen's dark blue eyes narrowed under her frown, and she blinked and looked down for a moment at the table full of magazines. When she glanced up again, Abby was seated at her own desk, carefully cutting out a purple flower.

I must be imagining things, Ellen thought, and she gazed again around the room. Mr. Fitz was bent over the desk of one of the girls who always had trouble spelling. He looked up, spotted Ellen on the sofa, and smiled a tiny, gentle smile at her.

Ellen finally pushed herself off the sofa and went on to the supply table. She chose a gold paper doily and some pink and white and green construction paper and carried it all back to her desk. She cut a white-petaled trillium and some bold green leaves and glued them onto the front of the card. While the card dried, she paged through her writing folder until she found the rough draft of her trillium poem. She read it carefully several times, and then tried to remember the trillium in the woods. She crossed off two lines of the poem and jotted down a few more phrases about the three-petaled flower. "First flowers of spring," she wrote. "Against the law to pick them." She thought a minute. "White, pretty," she added.

Ellen wrote and scratched out and erased and wrote again. Then she set aside her final draft and walked back to the supply table once more for a green calligraphy pen. Carefully she lettered "Happy Mother's Day, Mom" on the cover of the now-dry card. Inside she wrote her sensory verse.

Trillium
New and white against last November's brown
leaves
No one can hurt you
You are protected
Forever

Then she cut another trillium out of white paper, a replica of the one on the cover, but smaller, and glued it beneath the poem. She wiped up a blob of glue from her desk and went over to the classroom sink to wash her sticky hands. Then she cleared away the mound of paper scraps and put the open card in the middle of her desk. She sighed deeply and signed her card, "I love you, Mom. From Ellen."

Ellen walked home from school with Abby and Jen, and said nothing at all as her friends talked about the day at school and about their weekend plans. Ellen's mind was far away, on last year's Mother's Day. She and her mom and dad had gone to a fancy restaurant for a special brunch. They had joked about how after they became millionaires, they'd eat there all the time. Mom had laughed and said that she looked forward to leisurely lunches, instead of the quick sandwiches at Longfellow School, where she taught fifth grade. After brunch, they had walked in the grass along the river, in front of the restaurant, and Ellen had given her mom a handmade card with little clip-out coupons in it. The coupons said, "Wash the car," "Bake cookies," "Mow the lawn"—things Ellen would do for her mom.

Ellen's mom had sat down in the grass to open the card. She had taken off her Birkenstock sandals and stretched her long legs out in front of her. Her short brown hair with its few gray strands had tossed around in the breeze and her face, free of eye shadow or even lipstick, had looked with curiosity at the card. She had laughed in the warm spring wind and said, "Oh, here's my favorite—a back rub! I'll have that tonight." And she had taken Ellen's hands and looked at her and said, "Thank you for the lovely card and gift, Ellie."

Ellen felt Jen yanking on her sweatshirt.

"Ellen, did you hear that?" Jen was saying. "Abby's getting her ears pierced tomorrow." Ellen turned and stared at Abby.

Abby smiled and nodded. "Yup," she said. "*Everybody* has their ears pierced."

Ellen felt her own smooth earlobes and thought about how they'd laughed at Olivia's dangly earrings a month or two ago. "But, Abby," Ellen said, "I thought that you thought—"

Abby made a face and interrupted, "Oh, it's no big deal," she said. Her voice was scratchy, cross. "It's just time to join the real world." She kicked at a stone on the sidewalk and sent it bouncing off a white picket fence. Suddenly she smiled. "Anyway, how about a sleep over at my house tonight if my mom says okay?"

Ellen blinked at her friend. "Sure," she said. "I'll ask my dad." Ellen said good-bye to Abby and Jen and walked alone the last block to her house. She crossed her neighbor's yard and walked up her driveway along the thick bank of lilac bushes covered in dark purple buds. She stopped a moment at the circular flower garden to admire the bold reds and yellows of the tulips her mother had planted years ago, then walked up the sidewalk and climbed the wooden stairs to the wide porch. She headed toward the creaky swing that hung from the porch ceiling. She eased onto the swing, pushed it into motion, and pulled the newly made Mother's Day card out of her math book, where she'd tucked it to carry it home. Ellen let the gliding swing lull her as she read the words on the card.

I wish people were like trilliums, she thought. I wish *people* were protected forever.

Her tortoiseshell cat, Pepper, leaped suddenly from the porch railing to the moving swing. Pepper's loud purring indicated her disgust at having been left alone all day and her wish for immediate attention. Ellen made room in her lap for the big cat and scratched behind her ears. Pepper twisted her head to help Ellen find the itchiest spots, then settled down to sleep. Ellen rocked and stroked the cat a few minutes more. As she sat there, relaxed, an idea came to her.

"I know," she said quietly to the cat, and set her on the seat cushion of the swing. She held the card up to Pepper's face. "I know just the place to put the card." And she walked quickly toward the front door.

Ellen hurried through the front hall and stashed her backpack on the bench along the wall. Pepper followed so closely that Ellen nearly tripped in a tangle of cat feet. Carrying the Mother's Day card, she went to her parents' bedroom and slid open the door to her mom's closet. Dad hadn't done anything yet with Mom's clothes, and Ellen came to the closet frequently to feel close to her mother. As she opened the door, she inhaled deeply. Whiffs of sweet face powder and Oil of Olay, leather hiking boots, and school chalk dust wrapped around Ellen like a hug. Ellen slid the jeans jumpers, cotton skirts, and colorful vests down the rack of her mother's closet and pulled up a chair. Carefully she cleared a place on the floor among the sneakers, Birkenstock sandals, and school pumps and climbed up to check the top shelf.

Ellen shuffled through a pile of folded woolen sweaters and purses until her hand touched what she was after, the wooden box with a carved picture of mountains and evergreens, smelling of cedar. She sat in the middle of her dad's big bed and remembered the time she had seen her mom put a homemade valentine from her into the box. Another time, after an old silver locket had fallen apart at the hinge, her mom had said, "Well, into my history-mystery box with this one, Ellie," and she had slipped the antique treasure in. She had laughed then and added, "I call it that because someday, a hundred years from now, people will find it a mystery that I saved these bits of history." And then she had closed the box firmly and said, "But they're my most special memories."

Ellen traced her finger over the carved cedar mountains and trees on the cover of her mother's box. She held the box to her nose and breathed in the fresh cedar. She sniffed again and again, trying to hold the rich smell in her nose.

She raised the lid and looked at a Christmas card Dad had given Mom. It said, "Merry Christmas to my wife and to that wonderful bulge in the front." Ellen giggled. That bulge must've been me! she thought. Wow, this card is eleven years old! She looked farther into the box. There were some poems by Grandma and a school picture of Ellen from kindergarten. Ellen looked at the smiling blond little girl in the photograph, and remembered how she had insisted on wearing her velvet Christmas dress, even though picture day had been in September. Ellen found the first-grade valentine and the broken locket and a little plastic wrist strap that said, "Community Care Hospital. Anders. Girl. June 13, 1982." Ellen held the little bracelet with gentle fingers. She imagined that it once fit around her wrist. She thought about how small she must have been when her mom carried her out of the hospital. She thought about how safe she'd been then.

I'm glad Mom kept all this stuff, she thought. She lay back on her dad's bed and remembered all the times she had slept there with her mom and dad when she'd been small and afraid of the thunder. She held the little plastic wrist strap close to her cheek. I wish I had only thunder to be afraid of now, she thought. She lay quietly on the king-size bed, feeling small and alone.

Finally Ellen sat up on the bed and swung her feet to the floor. She put the things back into the box and then carefully lay her Mother's Day card on the top. Maybe Abby's right, she thought. Maybe Mom can see this box. Ellen wasn't sure what she believed in, religion-wise, but she had hopes about a lot of things. And one of her hopes was that there might be life after death.

Ellen sighed and began to close the cedar box. But then, beneath a tousle of cards and dried flowers, she noticed a book lying at the very bottom of the box. It was a dark green, leather-covered book, one Ellen had never seen. She hesitated a moment and then, curious, pulled it out. The book was untitled, and its covers were frayed and bent at the edges. Gold lines ran diagonally across the front and back. Ellen paused, and then slowly opened the book. She stopped, stunned at the words on the first page, "MY DIARY, 1962. Katie Hoffstrom."

She felt the way she had when she'd accidentally walked in on Grandma taking a bath, like an intruder. She gazed at the words and felt separated from the world.

Mom's diary! she thought. Holy cow! She read the same words over and over until Pepper's loud, hungry meowing brought her back to reality.

"Just a minute, Pepper!" Ellen said. She began to tuck the green book back under the treasures in the box, but stopped and pulled it out again. She set the book on her dad's bed, closed the cedar box, and tucked it back onto the shelf beneath the stack of sweaters. Then she returned the chair to her dad's desk, arranged the clothes and shoes into their original order, and carefully closed the closet door.

Green book under her arm, she went out to the kitchen to open a can of food for her hungry cat.

2

*E*llen scraped the cat food into Pepper's bowl, washed her hands, and walked slowly to the kitchen table, where she had set the diary. She lifted the green book gently and turned it over and over in her hands. She tried to imagine her mother as a girl her age, buying this book and opening it for the first time. Then, almost trembling, Ellen opened the front cover and read the title again, "MY DIARY, 1962." But she couldn't bring herself to turn the page. She put the book back on the table.

I'll get supper into the oven, she thought. Then I'll look. She went to the counter, where Dad always left a note.

Hi, Ellie, Hotdish in oven at 4:00. 350 degrees. Cut the long loaf and fix garlic bread. See you at 5:00.

He had signed it *Dad* in a squiggly script. A heart drawn in red marker decorated the final *d* in his name.

Ellen preheated the oven, then took the casserole out of the refrigerator and slid it onto the middle rack in the oven. She sliced several pieces of French bread, buttered them, and sprinkled them with garlic salt. She wrapped the bread in aluminum foil and set it aside to heat later.

Before her mom had died, Ellen had only helped with supper. Her mom, singing songs and saying silly things to the cat, would fly into the house, dump her school satchels and boxes on the dining-room table, and give Ellen a big hug.

"I can't even think until I get out of these monkey clothes," she would say about her "teaching" dresses and skirts. Then she would immediately change into jeans and an old sweatshirt, and would sigh with the pleasure of being home and in the kitchen. She would grab the bratwurst or codfish from the refrigerator, where it had been thawing all day, and she would start supper. Ellen would sit on the tall kitchen stool and tell her about playing softball in gym class and about being bored in math class. Or maybe she would just work on her social studies chapter review while her mom browned hamburger or peeled potatoes. Ellen would maybe scrape carrots or set the table, but she never would have guessed then that she could prepare a whole supper.

Ellen carried plates and glasses, silverware, and napkins to the table and set two places, sliding things around the green book. Finished, she looked at the table and realized that she'd put the diary in exactly the place where her mom used to sit at family meals. She quickly picked up the diary, then grabbed her homework from her backpack and headed for the TV room. She turned on the TV and opened her math book.

This was a new activity, too, one her mom hadn't allowed. "You can't think with that TV blaring, Ellie," she would say. But Ellen liked it on, and now she did homework in front of the TV every afternoon. She liked the noise and friendliness of it, and she knew Dad didn't worry about whether TV and homework went together.

She tucked the diary beside her on the sofa and pulled a colorful granny-square afghan around her shoulders and legs. I'll save the diary until later, she thought. The little book felt as big as a mountain against her hip. Ellen stared blankly at her math book. One part of her wanted to fling it to the floor and begin reading her mom's words without further thought. But another part of her felt sweaty with nervous worry about invading the secret world of her mom. She tried to concentrate on her assignment and her TV show.

Pepper jumped up and curled herself in the middle of Ellen's spiral notebook. Ellen scratched at Pepper's ears, leaned back against the sofa cushions, and turned to the page on division of decimals. "Pages 213–14," she wrote. "Problems 1–35." Mr. Fitz was adamant about his students identifying the assignment. She glanced at the problems and began with the simple ones, shifting her arm around the cat and glancing up at her favorite talk show.

23

Halfway into the assignment, and just as TV's Gloria Vanderslander was asking her guest why he planned to leave a million dollars to his Old English sheepdog, Ellen stopped doing decimals to try to remember the year in which her mother had been born. Careful not to disturb the purring cat, Ellen squeezed out of her cozy nest and went to the living room bookcase.

Reaching up, she hoisted the tattered, leather-bound family Bible off the shelf and onto the carpet. She turned to the second page, where her relatives from long ago were listed one after the other. Oliver Duffeneau, Agnes Decker, Hazel Johnson, Arthur Flector. She didn't know any of those people.

It's almost a poem, thought Ellen. Then she got to Grandma's name. Evelyn Duffeneau married Oswald Hoffstrom. That's Grandma and Grandpa Hoffstrom, she thought. Mom's parents.

Just beneath their names Ellen read, "Children: Anna, 1941; Eileen, 1947; Kathryn, 1950." And that's my mom! Ellen thought. Wow, 1950—that was a long time ago. She closed the Bible and put it back on the shelf.

Hmm, 1950. When did the diary start? she wondered. She ran back to the TV room, and as Gloria's guest strutted across the stage leading a huge gray and white shaggy dog, Ellen climbed back into her nest and opened the diary. "MY DIARY, 1962," it said.

The math was simple. Her mom had been twelve years old, one year older than Ellen was now. Ellen sat stock-still, suddenly chilled beneath the warm afghans. Oh my gosh, she thought, and she slammed the green book shut. It's so weird. She leaned back against the sofa, closed her eyes, and tried to think what to do, but she couldn't settle her thoughts. A minute later she heard the front door open.

"Hi, Ellie, I'm home!" Dad shouted.

Ellen thrust the green book into her math folder and piled her notebook and math book on top. Then, face red, she jumped up, rolling the cat into the tangle of afghan. She flicked off the TV and went out to meet her dad.

"Hi, Dad," Ellen called, her voice a little louder than usual, as she dashed into the hall.

"Hi, Ellie," Dad said, and grinned widely. "It smells good in here. Somebody's been cooking." He tossed his briefcase, full of essays by his college English students, onto the bench beside Ellen's backpack, and ruffled her hair. "You look"—he peered at her and then went on— "extra happy tonight. What's up?" He smiled at her again.

Ellen grinned back, and they walked into the kitchen.

"Oh, you know," she said as airily as she could. "It's Friday."

The phone rang, and she added, "That's Abby. She wants me to sleep over. Can I, Dad?" Ellen picked up the phone, put her hand on the receiver, and waited for her dad's answer.

"Sounds okay to me," he said. "If she checked with her mom and dad."

Ellen smiled. "He says I can come!"

After she finished making plans with Abby, Ellen grabbed her math book and the secret green book. Then she picked up her backpack and walked upstairs to her own room, which she thought of as her hideout. It was a small room her dad had built in the attic when they'd first moved, and it had sloping ceilings and a loft built in under the point of the ceiling. To save space, he had installed drawers that pulled out from the walls, and Ellen went directly to one of those drawers now. She pulled it out completely and set it on the floor, where it overflowed with socks and underwear.

Any time Ellen's dad built something or remodeled, he concealed messages or added secret places. He had put a hidden drawer into a large chest he'd built for Mom. The previous spring, before putting up wallpaper in the front hall, he'd insisted that they each write a message for the future on the newly stripped and cleaned walls, and sign their names and the date. Then he'd pasted up the new wallpaper, chatting about how things would have changed by the time somebody in the future removed it and found the messages.

Under Ellen's socks-and-underwear drawer there was a hidey-hole she loved. She tucked the diary in among the things already there—a two-dollar bill from Aunt Eileen, a map Ellen and Abby thought was a treasure map, a writing award from third grade, and a collection of four-leaf clovers. Jamming her socks and underwear together, she replaced the drawer.

Then Ellen threw her leg over the loft railing, pulled herself up onto her bed, and stretched out on her sleeping bag. Dad had said that the loft was too awkward for sheets and blankets, so for the last few months Ellen had been using her sleeping bag. She lay there on it, looking up at the ceiling, thinking, as she often did, about what the room would be like if it were upside down. She thought about the diary, lying in the secret hidey-hole, and wondered what to do about it.

I should read it, she thought. Since I found it, I should read it. If Mom could talk to me from heaven, or wherever she is, she'd tell me to read it. Ellen heard soft pit-pat steps and then a great scrabbling scramble as Pepper climbed to join her in the loft.

"But I'll bet she never meant for *anybody* to read it, *ever,*" Ellen whispered aloud to Pepper. "If Mom were here, alive," Ellen said, "and if I found the diary, I'd say, 'Mom, look what I found! Can I read it, Mom, please, can I?' And what would she say, Pepper?" She scratched Pepper's gray and orange forehead.

"She'd say, 'Oh, sure, Ellie. It's just a silly old thing.'" Ellen lifted Pepper's whiskery face and looked into her green eyes. "Wouldn't she, Pepper?" Ellen started stroking the cat's back. "Or maybe, she'd say, 'Not a chance, Cookie—not my private diary!'" She leaned against her pillow and Pepper spread out to sleep on Ellen's stomach. "But why would it matter now?"

The supper bell woke her from a light doze and she went downstairs. The kitchen gleamed bright with late afternoon sun. Her dad slipped on a hot mitt and carried the casserole and French bread to the table.

"The sleep over tonight worked out well," he said as they sat down to eat. "There's an English department party I should go to."

"Well, I could've stayed alone, Dad," Ellen said, thinking that for a long time he hadn't gone out at all, except to work and to church, and even now he didn't seem eager. "You shouldn't miss things because of me." She frowned. "Other kids in sixth grade already baby-sit."

After supper, Dad brought bowls of tapioca pudding to the table—one of his favorite desserts. They ate quietly for a while. They both knew the real reason he stayed home was that he missed Mom.

"Dad," Ellen said, "Sunday is Mother's Day."

Dad looked at her over his last spoonful of tapioca pudding topped with strawberry jam from last summer's preserving.

"Oh," he said, his face suddenly lined, "I completely forgot." Mom used to tease him about being the original absentminded professor.

"Well, I forgot, too," Ellen admitted. "Until Mr. Fitz mentioned it today."

Dad got up and gave Ellen a giant hug. "I'm sorry, Ellie," he said. He held her a while. "I remember your mom's first Mother's Day," he said. He unwrapped himself from Ellen and leaned against the kitchen counter, staring across the room and out the long kitchen window at the redwood deck and picnic table.

"Why, what happened?" Ellen asked.

"Well, you'd been cutting teeth for several days," Dad said. "And you were one crabby baby. So on Mother's Day, Mom took a vacation from being a mom, and went out to lunch and to a movie, and shopped at the mall for a whole day."

"What happened to poor little me?" Ellen asked. She imagined herself alone in her crib.

"Oh, you were fine and safe, home with your daddy," he said. "You cried with your sore gums all afternoon, and when Mom came home, all smiles, and with a new dress, she found both of us pretty weepy!"

Ellen laughed. "Tell me about another Mother's Day," she said.

Dad ruffled his hand through her hair. "Maybe another time," he said. "Now let's get these dishes done, and maybe there'll be time for a game of backgammon before you go to Abby's."

3

*E*llen balanced her rolled-up sleeping bag on her shoulder as she walked from her end of the block along the sunset-lit homes to Abby's house at the other end of the street. Sometimes Ellen wondered how many times she'd slept over at Abby's since their first time, eight years ago. Except for her own house, no place felt as much like home as Abby's, and Ellen felt happy and eager to be inside the Wickerses' house. Abby opened the door, and her enthusiastic German shorthair, Greta, nearly knocked Ellen over with her greeting.

Abby's mom was sprawled on the sofa, reading the paper.

"Hiya, Ellie," she said. "How are you doing?"

"Hi, Anne," Ellen answered. "I'm okay." Abby's mom was like an aunt to Ellen. Or a second mother.

"When is Jen coming?" Ellen asked as she and Abby headed for the family room.

Abby helped Ellen roll out her sleeping bag next to the plaid one that was already there, and they sat down.

"Oh, they had company for dinner," Abby said. "And her mom wanted her to stay home."

The girls grinned at each other. It was like old times. Ellen was pleased, but she didn't say so.

Last year, in fifth grade, most of the girls in their class had suddenly seemed to grow up faster than Ellen and Abby. They put on lipstick and wore clothes like junior high students, and they teased Ellen and Abby for jumping rope. Or worse yet, they just ignored them. When Jen moved in, wearing JCPenney jeans and getting all A's, they ostracized her, too.

The three girls—Ellen, Abby, and Jen—naturally banded together. They all loved to play long games of Monopoly, sometimes lasting a whole afternoon. When they'd admitted that they rented adventure movies about animals, such as *White Fang,* Olivia had said, "Why'd you want to watch a dumb movie about a dog?" Of course, there were some girls whose moms still walked them to school and who cried if the boys chased them. Even Ellen, Abby, and Jen ignored *them.* But the popular girls, in spite of their constant arguing and bragging, especially in front of the boys, seemed to be above everyone. Ellen, Abby, and Jen had invented a private name for them—the Dandy Dames.

By the end of fifth grade, Ellen, Abby, and Jen had become close friends. One time, sick of all the show-off stuff of those Dandy Dames, they had agreed to be true friends always, and they had cut long hanks of hair from close to their scalps and braided them into a single plait, rubber-banded at each end. Ellen's blond, Abby's brown, and Jen's nearly black hair were wound into a tight, secure rope.

"We have to have a pledge to go with it," Abby had said, holding up the three-colored braid. "O blond and black and brown braid," she said, voice low and solemn. Jen reached up and touched the hair, too. "We promise to be friends, unafraid," she said. "Come on, El." The three of them walked in a circle, right hands holding the braid high in the center. They spoke their pledge in chanting tones:

O blond and black and brown braid,
We promise to be friends, unafraid.

They had hidden the braid in an old Ritz cracker box and put it on the top shelf of Ellen's closet. Then they had sat on the rug in Ellen's bedroom and talked.

"True friends stick up for one another, no matter what," said Jen.

"And true friends don't talk about one another behind their backs," said Abby.

"Not even to another true friend!" said Ellen.

So far they'd never forgotten their friendship promise.

Ellen and Abby began a long, complex game of Monopoly. Later they made popcorn and watched an old movie. They tossed pieces of popcorn into the air and tried to catch them in their mouths. They laughed at a girl named Gidget, in a ruffly plaid swimsuit, who kept riding into shore on her surfboard with her hair perfectly curled and hardly wet. Then she would go and flirt with a young, handsome boy surfer, or some older guy who looked as if he needed a shave.

"Oh, is she ever dumb," Abby said.

"She's like the Dandy Dames," Ellen said, and she reached for another handful of popcorn.

"Oh, c'mon Ellen," Abby said. "Even they're not that bad." She reached across to the VCR and pressed the rewind button.

"No," said Ellen. She tossed a piece of popcorn into the air and caught it in her mouth. "They're a lot worse."

Finally, at ten-thirty, Abby's mom came in. "Into your beds, girls," she said. She tucked them both in, said good night, and turned out the light.

Ellen and Abby stretched out side by side in their sleeping bags on the thick carpet of the family room. Their two bags, Abby's plaid one and Ellen's army green one, lay close enough that the girls could reach out and grab hands if they wanted. It was in the cozy darkness that Ellen and Abby talked about important matters.

Abby turned on her side, facing Ellen, and rested her

head on her hand. "It was pretty mean of Mr. Fitz to do Mother's Day cards today," she said.

Ellen didn't respond right away. She nestled into the soft warmth of her down-filled sleeping bag, fluffed with double pillows beneath her head, and gazed around at the darkened family room in Abby's house.

"Well, other kids still celebrate Mother's Day," Ellen said slowly. She set her old teddy bear on the floor between the bags, and changed the subject. "Boy, would the Dandy Dames laugh at me for still using a teddy bear," she said, and both girls giggled.

Abby persisted. "Did you keep your Mother's Day card?" she asked.

"No," Ellen answered, and there was a silence. "Not really."

"What do you mean?" Abby asked.

"Well, I . . ." Ellen paused. "Remember when you said that maybe my mom would know about the card?"

Abby's face, curious, eyebrows raised, was visible in the beam of a streetlight shining through the window.

"Well, I decided to put the card in my mother's special box—something she used to call her history-mystery box."

"Oh, yeah, I remember that old carved box," Abby said. "So, did you?"

"Yes," Ellen said, "and by sheer coincidence—" She stopped and stared at Abby, her eyes suddenly wide and round. "Or maybe it was something more than coincidence. Anyway, at the bottom of the box I found something, almost like a gift from my mom."

Abby was very still, and she whispered, "What was it, El?"

"I found my mother's diary," Ellen replied. "From when she was just a year older than I am."

"Whoooaaa," whispered Abby. "That is something. Maybe it was meant to be. Did you take it?"

Ellen sat up in her sleeping bag. "Yes, I did. Why? Don't you think I should've?" she asked. "Would you have?"

"I don't know—it's so private," Abby replied. "I don't think I would read my mother's diary if I found it." She was silent for a while. "But if my mom had died, of course, then it would be different." She shifted in her sleeping bag and then suddenly turned to face Ellen. "I think you did the right thing, El," she said decisively.

Ellen smiled and relaxed. "Well, I haven't read it yet, Ab," she said. "I don't know if I should."

"Oh, I think you should. You're *supposed* to," Abby said. "The card and the box and your mom knowing and all—" her voice got louder, excited. "It's a way for your mom to still be with you."

"Maybe so," said Ellen. "So you *really* think I should read it?"

Abby's mother knocked on the door. "It's late, girls," she called. "Time to sleep." Her footsteps faded away.

"Yes!" Abby said to Ellen in a loud whisper. "And you

should start the day after tomorrow, on Mother's Day."

Ellen reached across and gave Abby a hug. "Thanks, Ab," she said, and leaned back into her thick, warm sleeping bag. "Good night," she said.

"Good night, El," answered Abby.

4

*O*n Mother's Day morning, Ellen woke up early, at six-thirty, too excited to sleep a moment longer. She stretched, climbed down from her loft, and got ready to go out. Then she opened her socks-and-under-wear drawer, lifted the green book out carefully from the hidey-hole, and tucked it under her jacket. She ran lightly down the stairs, and scooped up Pepper. Closing the front door quietly behind her, she walked down the block under a canopy of elm trees newly dressed in pale green.

Ellen headed for the woods at the end of the block. Pepper squirmed to get down and then trailed Ellen as she left the sidewalk and followed the path through the scrubby trees and across a bridge spanning a wide, shallow creek. Back in the woods, Ellen turned off the path and stepped over branches and piles of rotting leaves to her favorite spot, a place she and Abby had found three years ago. It was a room-sized space, formed by a huge tree that had fallen, leaving its root system standing upright. Washed by a thousand rain-storms, the meshed roots stood like a lacy wall. The roots, the long-broken trunk, and the brush of the tree's top formed a space—private, but open to the sun and the little creek.

Ellen went to the tree and spread her jacket on the dry, spongy moss. She leaned back against the root wall. She smiled at Pepper, who fell over her own feet trying to catch a butterfly. Then, taking a deep breath, Ellen lifted the diary gently in her hands and opened the cover. The old pages seemed thin, and the smudgy handwriting was blurry. Ellen felt as if she was opening King Tut's tomb, and she half expected violins to play or lights to flash.

Her heart beat faster as she turned to the first page and took a long look at it. It was pencil-written in a large, sprawly handwriting. The i's were dotted with little circles. Ellen smiled. She dotted her i's that same way sometimes, too. She read, imagining the skinny, wild-haired girl in the old photo album—her mom—writing in this book for the first time, more than thirty-one years ago.

December 29, 1962
Dear Diary,
How do you do. Let me introduce myself. My name is Kathryn Jean Hoffstrom, and I am twelve years old. My nickname is Katie to everybody but Dad. He calls me Bug because I'm the youngest. I have two older sisters, Annie and Eileen, but I'm the tallest child in my family. We live in a white house by Lake Superior, and my mom's a tele-

phone operator. Sometimes when she's working I call information just to see if I'll get my own mom. I can tell her voice. My dad's a mechanic, and we just bought a brand-new 1963 Chevy—yellow on top and black on bottom—our first-ever new car! Well, anyway, I'm tallest of the kids in our family and sometimes I feel that I'm taller than everyone in my whole 7th grade class, especially the BOYS. I'm kind of ordinary-looking, I guess, and until today I had straight brown hair. Mom gave me a Toni home permanent this afternoon and now my hair (rather, mop) is a royal mess. My best friends are Carole and Julie. We've been friends forever. It's winter now, and we love to go ice-skating. We skate every night we can, and I especially love to go because then I can see Freddie. Freddie is soooo handsome and he's as tall as me. The reason I can write in you tonight, Diary, is because I'm home baby-sitting. Uck. I forgot to tell you that I've got a foster brother who's been living with us forever—three years, ever since he was born. His name is Johnny and he shares my *bedroom* with me because Mom says it's the only place left for him to sleep. I baby-sit him a lot because Mom and Dad go to church all the time, and my sister Eileen has a job washing dishes at the hospital. My oldest sister Annie is out of high school and works in Minneapolis. So, anyway, I can't see Freddie tonight.

The entry ended with a little *sob* surrounded by teardrops. Ellen looked up at the creek and at Pepper, who had settled down in the leaves. She breathed deeply, flipped the page, and read on.

Thursday, December 30, 1962. 10:00 P.M.
Well, Diary, I'm home from skating (I got out of baby-sitting, for once). Boy, did I have fun!! Oh, Diary, Freddie skated with me! Wooooo!!!!! Wow, was I glad. He came up to me when I was skating with Carole and said, "Would you like to skate with me?" They were playing "Party Doll," which is the first song in the Top Ten and I love it. Oh, what a thrill!!!! He asked me to go home and have a party with him, but I said no, because I don't trust him. He also asked what I was going to be doing Saturday night. I said I had to baby-sit. Boy, am I a liar, eh?? You won't catch me partying with him! But maybe he wanted me to go to a movie with him. Nuts, Diary, I wish I could go to movies. I also wish I could wear lipstick, but no such luck when you go to my church. Gee, that gets a girl furious. I'll probably never be popular because of that. Oh, nuts.

Ellen closed the book, her feelings churning. *This can't be my mom,* she thought. She tried to imagine her mom skating at a rink with a boy. She could hardly even remember her mom as she'd looked last summer on their family camping trip to Lake Superior. What's all this stuff about boys? Ellen thought. She acted like that Gidget girl in the old movie Abby and I watched.

Ellen opened the diary again and reread the part about the church. I wonder why Mom's church wouldn't let kids go to the movies or wear lipstick, Ellen thought. Her mom had never mentioned that. She wondered if maybe that was partly why their family had attended the Unitarian church. Some Sundays they didn't go to church at all. They just went for a walk in the woods together. Her dad called it going to church under the Blue Dome.

Ellen stared at the mallard ducks on the shallow, spring-fed creek. She held the diary in her hands and rubbed her fingers over the leather covers. I won't read any more now, she thought. I need some time to think this stuff over. She stood up slowly and stretched, deciding at that moment to go to church with her dad. She wanted, on Mother's Day, to be at the church that her mother had loved. She brushed the sand and leaves off her jeans. "C'mon, Pep," she said. She tucked the diary under her T-shirt, and clutching it tightly to her ribs, headed home.

Dad was getting the thick Sunday paper off the porch as Ellen and Pepper walked past the two pink and white flowering apple trees and up the sidewalk.

"Hungry?" Dad asked. "I've got waffles going."

"Starved," said Ellen. "And I'm going to church today, too."

Ellen and her dad walked into the old schoolhouse

where the small group of Unitarian Universalists met. They said hello to several friends, then sat down to listen to a Bach violin suite played by a fellowship member.

Ellen looked up at her dad. She knew he hadn't always been Unitarian. "What religion were you and Mom when you were little?" she asked.

Dad leaned over. "I was Catholic and Mom was Pentecostal," he whispered, and then he sat up and looked straight ahead.

Ellen took the hint and was quiet.

The opening reading was printed on the program, but Ellen knew it by heart. It had been a favorite of her mother's, and Ellen had recited it at the funeral. The congregation stood now as church began.

> Look to this day for it is life,
> The very breath of life.
> In its brief course lie all the realities of your
>   existence,
> The bliss of growth, the glory of action, the
>   splendor of beauty,
> For yesterday is but a dream, and tomorrow only
>   a vision,
> But today, well lived, makes every yesterday
>   a dream of happiness,
> And every tomorrow a vision of hope,
> Look well, therefore, to this day.

Ellen let those words roll through her mind as the service about springtime and new life went on around her.

She leaned closer to her dad and let the dream of her mom fill her mind. She thought of the bike rides together and the snow creatures they had built and painted. She remembered skiing through the woods with her mom and swimming in Lake Superior together. She thought of sharing a bowl of popcorn and reading by the warmth of the fireplace. It was cozy in the little building, and Ellen's thoughts became real dreams. She awoke for the final reading that everyone said together.

After church Ellen and her dad unlocked their bikes, parked as usual under an apple tree near the church flower garden. They waved to friends as they wheeled their bikes onto the street.

"Can we go to Geraldine's Café for lunch, Dad?" Ellen asked.

Dad hopped onto his old green bike. "You bet," he said. "Delighted not to cook."

Ellen dipped a french fry into some mayonnaise and bit it in two.

Dad laughed. "You're the only person I've ever known, besides Mom, who eats french fries with mayo," he said.

Ellen grinned back.

"What was Mom like when she was my age, Dad?" she asked as she picked up her BLT sandwich.

"Well . . ." Dad thought for a minute, his face quiet and serious. "Of course I didn't know her then," he said. "Not till college." He smiled just a little. "But I've heard plenty of stories."

"Tell me!" Ellen said.

"Your mom was a tall skinny girl with unruly hair and big eyes," Dad said. "Have you ever seen that picture of her where she's hanging by her heels from a trapeze her dad made for her?"

"Yes, I remember it," Ellen said. "Grandma showed it to me. Grandma says that Mom was lively, that she did stuff she wasn't supposed to sometimes."

Dad smiled. "She was the youngest in the family and got away with everything, your Aunt Eileen always says. She had circuses in the garage and she visited the traveling band of gypsies that came to her town at crop-harvesting time. She had a yard sale once and sold a neighbor kid's toys."

"Was she in big trouble then?" Ellen asked.

"I don't know," Dad answered. He stopped talking to take a big bite of his chef salad. He chewed slowly and looked across the small table at Ellen. He put his hand on her wrist and squeezed it gently. "Are you worried about something?" he asked. "Is anything wrong?"

Ellen looked down quickly at her plate and took another fry with her free hand. "Well . . . I . . ." she said. "No. I just want to know about Mom."

"Okay," said Dad. "It's okay, Ellie." He let go of her arm and ate silently for a while. Then his eyes twinkled again and he bent across the table and whispered, "One time your mother and her friends tried to steal apples from a neighbor's orchard and the owner chased them with a shotgun." He laughed. "Ask Grandma to tell you some stories about Mom."

Dad finished his salad and picked up the bill. They left a tip and went out into the Sunday afternoon sunshine.

"I don't know about you, but I've got some papers to grade," Dad said as they rode along their block.

"I've got something important to do, too," Ellen said, and as soon as they got home, she picked up the meowing Pepper from the doorstep, went directly up to her room, and yanked open her socks-and-underwear drawer.

5

Ellen slipped the diary out of its hiding place and leaped onto her loft. She opened the book to the third page, then leaned back against her pillows.

Friday, December 31, 1962
Dearest Diary,
This afternoon Carole, Julie, and I went skating. Freddie had band practice so he didn't come up to the rink. All the kids know who I like. They say he likes me, too. I hope it's true . . .

Ellen stopped reading for a moment and stared up at the pointed ceiling of her bedroom. I sure don't understand what the big deal is with this Freddie, she thought. No girls I know like boys so much. Ellen's mind reviewed the girls in her class—Abby, Jen, some other girls, shy and quiet, practically invisible—and then it stopped, stalled, at one little gang. Of course the Dandy Dames are always talking about the boys, always putting on colored lip gloss, and smiling lovey-dovey at the tall, athletic boys. But they're the Dandy Dames. She opened the diary again.

Well, Di, tonight is New Year's Eve. In about four hours it will be 1963. I don't know yet what to do over midnight. What do you think, Diary? I'd watch TV if our family had it, but no such luck. Now I've got to make my New Year's resolutions and TRY to live up to them! Okay, here they are:

1. I'm going to try to be nicer to Johnny. (But it's almost impossible. What girl could stand to share her room—her SANCTUARY—with a bratty three-year-old who is spoiled rotten and not even her real brother?)

2. I'm going to stop arguing with Mom about stuff church doesn't allow. (But I'll NEVER understand why wearing lipstick is a sin! Why are red lips sinful? And movies? What does God have against movies? And school dances? And TV? And even comic books! We have to hide ours when the minister comes to visit!)

3. I'm not going to let Freddie know I like him so much. (Ho, ho, ho.)

4. I'm not going to fight as much with Eileen. (IF she's nice, that is.)

5. I'm—

Oh, that's enough for 1963!

Ellen let the green book rest on her chest. She thought about the times her mom had mentioned Johnny and about a faded snapshot her mom had shown her. In it her mom had stood in a long, blue wool coat. Beside her, on tiptoe, had stood a blond four-year-old boy dressed in tan snow pants and a fuzzy brown jacket.

"That was the day his mother took him and they moved to Idaho," Mom had said. "I even kind of missed the little devil." She had laughed.

Ellen thought about her mom's church, where movies and lipstick and comic books were considered sins. There was a girl in school who couldn't wear a Halloween costume because of her religion. And last year there'd been a boy who couldn't say the Pledge of Allegiance because his church didn't allow it. Could Mom's church have been like those?

She lifted the book and reread the last line. I wonder if she kept any of those resolutions in 1963, Ellen thought. She had just turned the page to continue reading when she heard familiar voices on the sidewalk below her open window.

"Ellie, come on out," called Jen.

"It's important," added Abby.

Ellen put her face to the screen. "Be right there," she called. She tucked the diary into her sleeping bag and slid over the edge of the loft.

"What's up?" she asked as she jumped from the porch to the grass.

Abby frowned. "It's the Dandy Dames," she said slowly.

"Yeah," said Jen. "They're having a boy-girl party on Friday, and guess what?"

Ellen broke a twig off the lilac bush that edged their yard. "My guess is that we're the only ones besides the real geeks who aren't invited." She laughed and reached down to scoop up Pepper, who was meowing and rubbing at her leg. "Who cares about those Dandy Dames? On Friday that phony-baloney Olivia was bragging on and on about how *expensive* her new sneakers were." Ellen strutted around, modeling her ratty old sneakers. "Doesn't that just drive you crazy? Boy, I'd like to—" Ellen stopped talking as she realized that her friends weren't responding.

Abby and Jen stood quietly, and Abby stared at the ground. Ellen looked at her friends. "That's it, isn't it?" she said. "We're not invited?"

Abby's voice was small. "That's partly true," she said, and she looked up, a little smile on her face. "I was invited, Ellie."

Ellen's mouth fell open. "That's crazy," she said. "Why would they ever ask any of us? They know you wouldn't want to go to their stupid old party." She stared at Abby.

Abby's face darkened to a red flush.

"I don't know why they asked," she said. "But I thought I might go." She started to smile, then covered her mouth with her hand.

The girls stood silent a long time, and Pepper finally leaped from Ellen's arms to chase after a mayfly on the grass at their feet. For the first time in her friendship with Abby, Ellen couldn't think of anything to say. She shifted from foot to foot, then reached down once more to pick up the cat.

Jen remained absolutely silent.

Abby broke off a large bloom from the lilac bush and put it to her nose. She looked up briefly at her two friends. "Well, I have to go," she said. "My family's going over to my grandma's for the afternoon." She turned and started toward her home. "Bye," she said.

Ellen and Jen watched her go.

"Bye," Jen called.

Ellen didn't say anything.

Ellen and Jen stood side by side, staring at Abby as she walked quickly away, down the block. They waited until she'd turned off the main sidewalk and disappeared into her own yard.

"I can't believe it," said Ellen. "I can't believe that Abby'd go to *their* party."

"I think she broke our braid pledge," Jen said.

"I think so, too," said Ellen. "I don't think it's possible to be friends with us *and* the Dandy Dames."

"Let's go get the braid," Jen said. Pepper leaped away at the sudden motion.

The girls ran into the house and up to Ellen's room. Ellen reached high into her closet and pulled down the Ritz cracker box. Jen opened the flaps and lifted out the woven black, brown, and blond braid. She felt the smooth, twisted strands and handed it to Ellen. Ellen was holding and bending the braid when she heard the garage door open and the car door slam. Then she heard the back door open and her dad's yell.

"Hey!" he said. "You home, Ellie?"

Ellen put the braid back into the box. "Up here, Dad," she called. "In my room, with Jen." Jen slid the cracker box back onto the closet shelf, and the girls went out into the hall.

Dad stood at the bottom of the stairs. "What're you girls doing inside on such a beautiful day?" he asked. "Let's bike to the Dairy Queen and get a Dilly Bar."

Ellen and Jen looked at each other and smiled. "Okay," said Ellen. "Let's." They followed Ellen's dad into the garage. "But I'll have to give Jen a ride to her house to pick up her bike," she said.

"Sure," said Dad. He wheeled his bike out onto the driveway. "Where's the third musketeer today?" he asked. "Would Abby like to go to Dairy Queen?"

Jen sat on the crossbar and hung onto the handlebars. Jen and Ellen looked at each other again. They both frowned. "We don't know," said Ellen.

"She's gone somewhere," said Jen. And they biked carefully onto the quiet street toward Jen's house a few blocks away.

6

*E*llen and Abby walked to school together on Monday morning, as they had since the first day of kindergarten. Jen joined them at her corner. Everything was the same, but everything was different. Ellen thought about the party, but didn't say anything about it. Abby didn't ask about the diary. In fact, she hardly said a word.

When they reached the playground at school, Olivia and Heather, another Dandy Dame, rushed up to them. "Hi, there," Olivia said, glancing briefly at Ellen and Jen. Olivia never used a person's name when she greeted a non-friend. Olivia grabbed Heather's arm and the two girls turned immediately to look at Abby. Heather's long, light hair was in a French braid, not a strand out of place. Olivia's short brown hair curled around her ears and over her collar. Her earrings were genuine turquoise stone set in sterling silver. Both girls stood half a head taller than anyone in the sixth grade, boys included.

"Abby," Olivia said, her back to Ellen. "I hope you've decided to come to my party. It'll be a pool party and there'll definitely be boys."

Abby blushed, glanced at Ellen and Jen, then moved

away with Heather and Olivia. Ellen didn't hear her answer, but she heard the three girls giggling and shrieking.

Later Ellen slumped in her desk, math book open.

"Ellen?" Mr. Fitz touched her shoulder.

Ellen was startled. She sat up quickly, and could hear her classmates laughing.

"Ellen, will you simplify this math expression?"

She stared up at the board.

$$3 \times 3 - 3 + 12 \div 3 + 3 \times 8 = 72$$

Ellen was confused and glanced around, hesitating.

Jen leaned forward in her desk behind Ellen. "Ellie," she whispered, "Olivia thinks the answer is 72. You're supposed to correct her mistake. Wake up!"

Ellen walked to the board and picked up the chalk.

$$3 \times 3 - 3 + 12 \div 3 + 3 \times 8 =$$

Automatically she wrote the next steps.

$$9 - 3 + 12 \div 3 + 3 \times 8$$
$$9 - 3 + 4 + 3 \times 8$$
$$9 - 3 + 4 + 24$$
$$6 + 4 + 24$$
$$10 + 24$$
$$34$$

"Right," Mr. Fitz said. Ellen put the chalk down and walked toward her desk.

"Miss Brilliant America," Olivia whispered loudly as Ellen passed her. The kids nearby laughed. Ellen turned sharply and looked at Olivia, ready to shoot back a nasty remark. But when she saw that Olivia sat rigid at her desk, eyes dark and face frozen, she changed her mind.

As Ellen sat down she felt Jen pat her shoulder. "Forget those jerks," Jen said.

Ellen turned to smile at Jen, but she stopped halfway around and looked across the room at Abby, who sat staring at her math book, red faced.

The morning dragged by. Math ended and science began, and Ellen wrote up Friday's rocks and minerals experiment as though she were a robot. Just before lunch, she took the regular spelling pretest and was surprised when she made mistakes.

Finally the 11:50 bell rang and Ellen trudged to the gym, now a cafeteria. The long tables with attached benches fit smoothly into the walls when it was time for volleyball or tumbling or basketball. But at midday, the custodian pulled the tables and benches down and across the shiny gym floor. The cook opened the tall serving windows into the kitchen, put out stacks of trays and bins of silverware, and the gym turned into a noisy, colorful, crowded cafeteria.

Ellen and Jen reached for lunch trays, stopped for milk cartons and straws, and then walked to one end of a long table. As they picked up grilled cheese sandwiches, they saw Abby come in from crossing-guard duty and hang her bright orange patrol belt on a hook in the hall.

"I still can't believe that Abby would be friends with Olivia Von Cracken," said Jen. "What's going on?"

Ellen stared at Abby. The tiny gold starter earrings in Abby's ears seemed as big as marbles to Ellen. "I'm not sure," she said. "But Abby's been acting different since her parents joined the country club where Olivia's family goes." She picked up her sandwich. "It makes me so furious."

Abby walked quickly toward their table.

"Hi, you guys!" she said, and sat down, acting as if everything was the same as ever. She picked up a french fry and dipped it into the ketchup. "Boy, you could break your teeth on these fries, they're so hard." She laughed.

It was quiet at the table.

Abby opened her milk and put the straw in. "Hey, what's with you?" she asked, slurping milk.

Ellen looked directly at Abby. "What's with us?" she said sarcastically. "What's with *you?*"

Jen shifted around on the bench. "What's with all the cozy-up to the Dandy Dames stuff?" she said.

Abby looked down at her sandwich, picked it up, then put it down. "Oh. Well . . ." she said, eyes on her tray. "Maybe we shouldn't call them that. They're not so bad, you know."

"What?!" Jen grabbed Abby's arm. "Not so bad? All they think about is clothes, and they hardly ever get their homework done on time. They hide in the bathroom because they don't want to go outside at recess. And they flirt with boys and act like big shots." Jen's voice broke, and she gasped. "They just think that the only people who matter in the world is them and their friends! You always said—"

Ellen interrupted. "All I want to know, Abby, is if you're going to their party," she said. "All I want to know is if you're going to join the totally all-time creepiest snobs in the universe."

Abby frowned and Ellen, who knew her so well, watched her eyes dart from left to right and back. Her lips quivered, too. Ellen had seen Abby worried and confused many times in their friendship, but never to this extent. She hadn't even looked this addled last summer when she'd broken her family's bay window with a boomerang they'd been throwing around.

Abby didn't answer. Trays in hand, Olivia and Heather strolled toward their table.

"Well, are you going?" Ellen said loudly. "*Are* you, Abby?"

The two tall girls stopped beside Abby, their backs to Ellen and Jen. Ellen stared glumly at Heather's long, thick honey blond hair. Her own hair felt so fine, she was afraid her skull showed through.

"Hi, Abigail," Olivia said. "We're planning the games for the party. Want to help?"

Abby wriggled on the cafeteria bench and averted her face from Ellen and Jen.

"And the music," Heather added. She tossed her long braid back over her shoulder. "We've got some great ideas for the music."

Abby finally jumped up from the bench, gave a little shake of her body, and then suddenly lifted her head high. Her back seemed taut. The frown on her red face turned into a rigid smile as she looked at Heather and Olivia.

"Sure, I'd love it," she said. She touched her hair, patting it in a way Ellen had never seen her do before, and turned to Ellen and Jen. She bent low over the table, over the grilled cheese sandwiches, french fries, canned peaches, and milk cartons. Her back to Heather and Olivia, she looked directly at Ellen and Jen. "Yes, I am going to the party," she said quietly. Her eyes were dark and seemed wet, ready to spill over.

"Come on to our table," said Olivia, "and we'll plan during lunch."

Abby turned slowly and looked from Ellen and Jen to Olivia and Heather. She had a smile on her mouth, but her forehead was wrinkled into a frown. "See you guys later," she said, and turned back to them adding, in a pleading whisper, "Can't I be friends with them and with you both?" She picked up her tray and followed the other girls.

Ellen bit into her sandwich with a mighty chomp. "Some wonderful true friend," she said to Abby's retreating back. But only Jen heard.

7

Ellen and Jen both had safety-patrol duty after school. When they had helped all the students across the street, they stashed their long poles with the little yellow flags on the ends in the hall closet and took off their bright orange patrol belts. Then they walked home together in almost complete silence.

"What word did you go down on in the spelling bee?" Jen asked.

"Reconciliation," Ellen answered.

Silence.

"What're you doing tonight?" Ellen asked.

"Baby-sitting my little cousins," Jen answered.

Silence.

"Want to go to the new Disney movie with me?" Jen asked.

"Okay," Ellen answered.

Silence.

"How about the Saturday matinee?" said Ellen.

"Okay, it's a deal."

Their slow walking and hesitant talking finally took them close to their houses.

"Bye, Ellie," Jen said when they reached the corner, and she turned to walk toward her home.

"Bye." Ellen watched a moment as Jen walked away. The sky was dark, and Ellen could hear thunder. She walked quickly through the streets of her neighborhood and then ran the last half block when the rain began to fall.

Pepper scooted out from beneath the porch, where she had been hiding from the rain, and rubbed against Ellen's legs as she pulled out her key to unlock the front door. Ellen set the mail and her backpack on the hall bench and went to the kitchen. Dad's note was on the counter.

Hi, Ellie,
Homemade pizza tonight. Please mix up the dough and let it rise.

Love, Dad

Ellen measured a teaspoon of dry yeast into a bowl and added a cup of warm water. She knew this favorite recipe by heart. She added the flour, gradually mixing it into a doughy ball, covered it, and put the bowl on the counter.

Then she washed a stalk of celery, filled the center hollow with peanut butter, and skipping her usual TV-homework routine, went directly to her room. I don't need a talk show today, she thought. I have my own problems. She took a big bite of celery with peanut butter, and slowly opened the diary, careful not to get peanut butter on it. The familiar warmth and excitement of being close to her mom spread through her mind as she turned to the place where she had left off and began reading.

Sunday, January 2, 1963. 9:30 P.M.
Hi Diary,
I'm home from skating, Diary. Freddie skated with me twice! He skated alongside of me almost all evening. Whenever he would come up next to Carole and me, Carole would go. I guess she felt like a 5th wheel! I told Freddie to skate with Carole and he said he would if I would give him something. I offered him a bus token, but he said he didn't want it in money . . . IN OTHER WORDS HE WANTED A KISS. I flat refused him. When I was skating with him he kept squeezing my hand. I told him to quit, but he wouldn't.

Ellen rolled onto her side on the bed and set the last chunk of celery on the little shelf by her loft. Suddenly she didn't feel hungry for her favorite snack. Mom was only a year older than I am, she thought. How could she have been so different from me? Ellen's thoughts shifted from the diary to Olivia's party and the boys who'd be there. She imagined Abby, in her new earrings, talking with Kyle Bloss. She saw her laughing with Olivia and not even thinking about Ellen.

Probably my mom would've been invited to a party

like that in her day, Ellen thought. She rubbed her eyes and stared, unseeing, across the room at her cluttered bulletin board. Then she turned back to the diary.

Monday, January 3, 1963
Hello, Diary, ole pal,
I'm mad, mad, mad, MAD!! Freddie was real unfriendly today in school. He didn't smile at me once. Boy-oh-boy, tomorrow in school, so help me, I'm going to be real unfriendly to him so he'll go to Madison feeling bad. Ha, that's a laugh and a half. He wouldn't feel bad. He'd feel GLAD!! The S-N-O-B. I suppose he thinks he's playing hard-to-get. Well, Di, if that's the case, he isn't too far ahead of me. I know how to play H.T.G. ALSO!

Mom sure didn't have the same kind of problems that I have, Ellen thought. Pepper sniffed at the peanut butter celery.

Tonight Mom and Dad went to a concert that the high school band is putting on. Freddie plays in the band even though he's just in 7th grade. I wish I could have gone since he was in it. He asked me last night if I was coming. Tough luck—of course I had to baby-sit. It wouldn't even be so bad if we had TV, so I could watch "Inner Sanctum" or "Your Hit Parade," the way Carole gets to when she baby-sits her little brother. Nuts, Di, no TV!

Ellen closed the diary and her eyes at the same time. She lay on her sleeping bag, stunned to realize whom her mom reminded her of. She climbed down from the loft and tucked the diary into the hidey-hole. Then she finished eating the piece of celery and trudged downstairs.

She went to the bookcase and looked through the row of photo albums lining the bottom shelf. One was labeled "Days Gone By." Ellen pulled it off the shelf. She had looked at it many times before with her mom and dad. She paged through the thick book until she came to "Junior High School." Ellen looked from picture to picture at funny, silly shots of her mom and friends posed in pajamas at a sleepover, in swimsuits at the beach, on bicycles. They look so sure of themselves, Ellen thought. She put away the photo album. How weird, she thought, and wondered whether to laugh or cry. My mom was kind of a Dandy Dame.

Ellen leaned against the bookcase, suddenly overwhelmed by a longing for her mom—her *real* mom, not the twelve-year-old in the green diary.

I wish this thing with Abby had happened last year, in fifth grade, when I still had my mom, she thought. So I could've asked Mom what to do. Then she shook her head violently. No, that's not true. Then I wouldn't have had Abby as my friend when Mom died.

She thought about how Abby had stayed overnight with her on those awful days before the memorial service, how Abby had sat right beside her at church in an area reserved for family. She remembered the times she had gone on little trips with Abby's family—to visit Abby's grandma, to see the orange-and-red autumn leaves, even to the garden shop. And how Abby had helped her and her dad choose the Christmas tree at the tree farm, haul it home, and trim it.

No, she thought. I couldn't have made it without Abby. Ellen pulled her legs up to her chin for a minute and put her head down on her knees. Darn that Abby, she thought. How could she desert me now for those, those . . . Dandy dope dumbheads! Finally, she stood up. And how could my mother have been a Dandy Dame?

Ellen walked slowly into the kitchen to set the table. Then she went to get her backpack in the front hall and, for the first time in months, sat at the desk in the living room to do her homework.

8

*E*llen picked up a piece of pizza. Slices of pepperoni, sausage, and black olives smothered it. The crust was thick, and a double layer of cheese dripped over the edge. Pizza had been Dad's specialty even before Mom had died. Usually Ellen loved her dad's pizza, but tonight she ate slowly, with a frown on her face.

"You okay, Ellie?" Dad asked when he noticed. "Are you sick?"

Ellen sighed, thinking about Abby and the party, the green diary, and her mother, a Dandy Dame of the 1960s.

"I don't think you'd understand, Dad," Ellen said.

"Well, try me," Dad said. "I was a sixth grader once." He picked up his fourth piece of pizza. "It was a long time ago, but I still remember." He chuckled.

Ellen felt the anger at Abby suddenly burst out at her dad. "You were never a sixth-grade *girl,* Dad," she said. "You just don't know how I feel . . . with friends and everything!" She set the barely nibbled pizza down on her plate.

Dad put his pizza down, too. He looked closely at

Ellen. "You having friend troubles, Ellie?" he asked. "Can you tell me?"

Ellen set her napkin by her plate and pushed her chair away from the table. "I don't feel like talking. I guess I don't feel so great, Dad," she said. That was true. "Maybe I'm just tired."

Dad slowly picked up his pizza again. "Boy, kiddo, if you're too tired to eat Dad's famous pizza, you're tired!" He bit into the pepperoni and sausage. "I'll do dishes tonight," he said. "Why don't you just watch TV and relax?"

Ellen stood up. "Okay, Dad," she said. "Thanks."

Dad called to her as she left the room. "Ellie!"

Ellen stopped and turned around.

"If you want to talk sometime, I'm here."

"Thanks, Dad," she said, nodding, and walked into the TV room.

Ellen sat on the old striped green-and-white sofa and flipped the channels from news to commercials to cartoons to a religious interview. She watched a few minutes of a game show, but she didn't absorb a thing. Her mind was flicking around, too, searching for an idea. Suddenly she hopped up from the sofa and turned off the TV. She took the stairs to her room two at a time and searched recklessly through the bookshelf. Grabbing a book, Ellen ran downstairs.

"I'm going to Abby's to return a book," Ellen said to her dad.

He was swabbing the counters. "You got better in a

hurry. What's up?" He looked at her sharply, his bushy eyebrows raised in question.

Ellen held up the Nancy Drew book for him to see. *The Whispering Statue* by Carolyn Keene.

"I think she needs this book," she said. "I'll be right back." She ran out the door before her dad could respond, and holding tightly to the book, borrowed months ago, raced down the block.

I just have to talk to Abby, she thought, but she slowed her steps halfway down the block. But what can I say? She stopped and leaned against a huge oak trunk and thought of ways to begin.

"Abby, are you still my friend?" she tried out loud. She picked at the bark of the old tree. "Abby, remember our braid and our vow?" She rubbed the bark into dust in her free hand. "Abby, you're the only person in the world who knows I have my mother's diary." Ellen sighed. "Abby, what's happening?"

It's ridiculous to be nervous, Ellen thought. She tossed the bark dust on the lawn and brushed her hand clean on her jeans. We've been friends for such a long time. Ellen felt Pepper at her ankle so she bent to pick her up. Holding the cat and the book, she continued down the block.

When she reached the steps of Abby's house, she heard voices and laughter. The Wickerses have company, she thought. I'll go around to the side porch. As she put her foot on the first porch step, she heard a distinctive shriek of laughter and saw a familiar girl.

Oh, no, Ellen thought. That's Olivia. Ellen turned to duck behind the bushes. But it was too late. Olivia had spotted her.

"Hi, there," Olivia called. "Look who's here, Abigail," she said, and she gave the floor a little push with the toe of her fancy, high-topped, white-and-green sneaker, setting in motion the porch swing where she and Abby sat. Ellen stared at the familiar porch and at Abby and Olivia sitting on the creaky, comfortable swing where Ellen had sat with Abby ten million times.

Ellen stood, a statue with a book in one hand and a wriggling furry animal under one arm. Abby, her face red, jumped off the swing and went to meet Ellen.

"Hi, Ellie," she said. She stood at the porch rail and looked down at Ellen in the grass. "We're, uh, we're just . . ."

Ellen forced herself to move, and she stuck out the hand with the book in it, embarrassed that she needed this inane excuse to see her oldest friend and especially mortified that Olivia was a witness.

"I was just returning this book," she said. "Thanks." She turned quickly, just as Abby's mom pulled up with a carful of groceries.

"Oh, hi, Anne," Ellen said. She stalled, trying to look normal, while Mrs. Wickers climbed out of the station wagon.

"Hi, Ellie," Abby's mom said. She set a grocery bag down on the car. "I bought some ice cream. Come on in, and you girls can make sundaes."

"Uh, no, thanks," Ellen said. "I have to, uh, do the dishes."

She saw Olivia take the book from Abby's hand and laugh as she read the title. Ellen crossed the grass toward home, forcing herself to walk slowly, with as much dignity as she could salvage. She heard Abby laugh, too, and then the creak of the old swing as the girls rocked.

As Ellen hugged Pepper to her chest and began to run, she heard Abby's voice, clear and happy. "C'mon, 'Livia, let's go make hot fudge banana splits!"

Ellen ran home and up to her room. She climbed into her loft, punched her pillow over and over, and then lay still, staring out at the spring leaves on the tall maple.

9

 Ellen's homework seemed like the least important thing in the world that night. The commutative, associative, and distributive properties of her math assignment made her dizzy. She just stared at her South American project, and even the water-powered electricity experiment she was building for the spring science fair didn't hold her attention.

Ellen pushed the books and papers aside, went downstairs, and called Jen. Jen sounded happy to hear from her.

"Hi, El," she said. "Did you get the math stuff?"

"Kind of," Ellen said. "But I just can't think about math."

"Or social studies or anything," Jen said. "I know what you mean."

"Jen," said Ellen, "Olivia was at Abby's house tonight."

"She was?" Jen said. "They're getting more buddy-buddy every day."

"They were laughing and joking and I felt like a complete idiot when I went to return a book," said Ellen. "I couldn't get out of there fast enough."

"Ellen," Jen said suddenly. "Do you realize what we're doing?"

"No," Ellen said. "What?"

"We're breaking a rule from our braid ceremony. We're talking about the one who isn't here."

A burst of sound came from Ellen, half snort, half laughter. "Breaking the rules!" she said. "Abby's broken *all* the rules. Her hair shouldn't even be in the braid anymore."

The girls talked a long time, until Ellen's dad walked through the kitchen and pointed at the clock.

"In a minute, Dad," Ellen whispered and made a face, trying to listen to Jen's idea for walking to school the next day. Dad went into the TV room.

"Sounds great, Jen," Ellen said. "Abby'll never figure out which way we went. Why should we walk with her?"

"See you tomorrow, El," said Jen.

Ellen said good night to her dad and went upstairs. She brushed her teeth, climbed into her bunk, and reached for the comfort of her mother's diary. She slowly read through two entries of boyfriend problems and baby-sitting woes.

Ellen smiled, closed the diary, and curled around Pepper, who had joined her in the loft. She meant to get up in a minute to put away the diary and turn out the lights, but the closeness of it near her chest made her feel secure, and she lay still, thinking about her mom.

What would *you* do, Mom? she thought. What

would *you* do, Katie Hoffstrom? She imagined Katie, who seemed so brave and talkative, walking into Mr. Fitz's classroom. She wondered what it would be like if one of Katie's best friends—Carole maybe—got all buddy-buddy with Olivia. She thought about Olivia seeing Katie and saying, "Hi, there," as if Katie didn't have a name and didn't really exist.

Then what, Katie Hoffstrom? Ellen thought. Then what, Mom? Ellen hugged the book closer. Would you be so cheerful then? Would you punch Olivia? Would you bug Carole to be friends again? Would you forget Carole and just hang out with Julie? The questions and an image of a grinning, ice-skating girl swirled in Ellen's mind until she fell asleep.

Bright spring sunlight tilted across the walls. Dad was singing a silly old wake-up song that he and Mom always used to sing when Ellen was little:

Wakey, wakey, rise and shine,
Wakey, wakey, rise and shine,
Wakey, wakey, rise and shine,
Wakey, wakey, rise and shine,
Good morning, friend.

Ellen groaned at the goofy song.

"Good morning, Ellie," Dad said. "You were zonked out last night when I came in to turn out your light. I guess you *were* tired."

Ellen turned to her dad, smiling and still half-asleep.

Then she noticed that her dad had the diary in his hand, and her eyes widened. Uh-oh, she thought. Her stomach tightened and her heart revved up.

But Dad was grinning. "I see you found Mom's girlhood diary," he said.

Ellen sat up. She realized she had been holding her breath, and now she let it out in a whooshing sigh. "Oh, Dad, I thought you'd be mad," she said, and she told him how she found it.

Dad hugged her close when she talked about the Mother's Day card, and he stroked her hair. "Honey, it's fine," he said. "Mom always said she thought you'd get a kick out of reading her diary when you got to be the same age as she was then."

"But I'm a year younger," Ellen said.

Dad put the book on the sleeping bag beside Ellen. "Somehow I don't think that matters," he said. "Do you?" He leaned over to transfer a pair of jeans from the floor to a chair.

Ellen picked up the diary. "No," she said. "But, Dad?"

He looked up.

"She was so different from me," Ellen said. "So boy crazy and silly. Her problems were so . . . just so . . . well, not really problems."

Dad was quiet a minute. "Oh, she had problems, all right," he said. "But she had such a positive spirit, such optimism, that maybe she sounds silly in her journal."

"Dad?" Ellen said slowly. "Mom reminds me a little

of some girls in my class at school. Some girls I don't like."

He smiled. "I think your mom was a lot like any other eleven- or twelve-year-old in the whole world," he said, and he cupped his hand under her chin for a second. "Just trying to grow up." He stroked her hair out of her eyes. "And it's never easy," he added. "That girl in the diary was a pretty special girl. Keep reading. She liked a lot more than just boys."

Dad turned to leave the room. "Are the girls in school part of the friend trouble?" he asked.

Ellen sat up in her loft. "Yeah," she said. "Kind of."

Dad turned back and put his hand on the edge of the bunk. "Well, maybe even they're not as bad as you think," he said. "Give yourself a chance to like them." He ran his hands through Ellen's snarled morning hair. "Get up now, El," he said, "and let's get some corn-flakes into you."

*E*llen and Jen did alter their route to school and met at a new spot for the rest of the week.

"This was a good idea, Jen," Ellen said as the girls met fifteen minutes before they usually did, in an alley a block away from their regular meeting place. They cut through a long parking lot and two backyards to come out near the school. They shuffled along the blocks, their talk quiet, until they approached the playground. Then, in unspoken agreement, they hid their glum spirits with loud voices, swinging their arms and smiling as they talked.

"I hear the new dinosaur movie is coming out in a couple of weeks," said Ellen. "Should we go to it together?"

"Sure," said Jen. "Hey, El, you know what? My hamsters had babies *again!*"

The girls discussed Jen's swim team and plans for summer vacation. They talked about school assignments and Mr. Fitz. As they entered the playground, they saw a group of girls gathered by the building and Jen spoke up loudly. "Hey, El, did you hear about the kid who was run over by a steamroller?" She bent over and whispered the punch line to Ellen, and they both laughed as if it were the most hilarious joke they'd ever heard. They very carefully steered clear of even mentioning Abby.

A few days later, on the night of Olivia's party, Ellen and Jen had a sleepover at Jen's house. They spread out their sleeping bags, made popcorn, and watched a movie. True to the braid vow, they carefully avoided talking about Abby, but when they didn't laugh even at the funniest parts of the movie, Ellen spoke up. "I wonder what it's like," she said, her voice quiet.

Jen knew exactly what Ellen was talking about. "I wonder, too," she said. "What do you think they do at their parties?"

"Maybe they dance," Ellen said.

"Or they play kissing games," Jen said.

Ellen and Jen speculated for a long time while the movie played on, ignored. When they noticed the credits rolling by at the end, they switched off the TV, carried their bowls into the kitchen, and crawled into their sleeping bags. They talked until late, and when they heard Jen's mom and dad coming home, they pretended to be asleep.

A couple of weeks after the party, as Ellen cut through backyards along her new route to meet Jen, she heard clomping footsteps and Abby's voice behind her.

"Ellie," Abby called. "Wait a sec. I'm trying to catch up." Abby panted as she drew up next to Ellen. "I've been wondering which way you were taking. I've been looking for you and Jen."

Ellen stopped and turned back. "Hi," she said. She had been avoiding all contact with Abby at school, but now she looked carefully at her old friend. Abby seemed the same—hair in a long ponytail clinched with a pink elastic holder, faded jeans, big sweatshirt, freckly face—but somehow she looked different to Ellen, too. Older, maybe. Ellen couldn't tell what it was.

"So what's up?" Abby asked as she slowed down to catch her breath. She smiled widely and didn't wait for Ellen to answer. "Hey, El, do you have your South American report done? What a pile of work that is, eh?"

Ellen shifted her books again and glanced at Abby. "No," she said. "And yes."

Abby laughed at the silly answer, and Ellen laughed, too, though she hadn't intended to. Jen joined them at the new corner. She looked surprised to see Abby, but made no comment about it as they walked together, discussing the track meet and the math team. They talked about the science fair and the end-of-the-year awards ceremony. All the talk was neutral, and neither Ellen nor Jen asked Abby anything about her new friends. Abby didn't mention them, either. If strangers had been listening, they'd have thought the three girls were good friends.

We're fakes, thought Ellen.

When they walked onto the school playground, Jen headed for the sixth-grade door. "I have to go in early and work on my report," she said. "I forgot to take it home over the weekend."

"I'm on patrol duty," Abby said, and she hurried toward the office entrance.

Ellen sat down on a swing and set her books and folders in her lap. She swung gently back and forth, and thought about how odd it felt to have Abby be just a regular person, not a best friend. She pushed her sneakers into the dirt under the swing. It kind of reminds me of a divorce, she thought. She imagined it in the newspapers—"Best Friends of Eight Years Separate," the headline would say. "Ellen Anders and Abby Wickers, of Canton Court, friends of many years, have gone their separate ways."

Suddenly Olivia was right beside Ellen. "Hellooo, Ellen," she said, and she leaned against the steel poles of the swing set.

Ellen looked up, startled. Hello, *Ellen?* she thought. Olivia's saying something other than "hello, there"? Ellen didn't say a word. She just stopped her swing, held tightly to her books, and stared.

Olivia wrapped one leg around the steel pole and reached high up the pole with one arm. She put her other hand on her hip and leaned down toward Ellen on the swing. Her smile was wide and bright. Ellen caught herself smiling back and then stopped. What could Olivia want? she wondered. Maybe she needs help in math. I did help her before.

Olivia spoke then, her voice melodic and syrupy. "Wouldya like to go to Pinetown Mall with us on Saturday afternoon? We're all getting new jeans and sweaters at Richwell's Togs."

Ellen gulped down a lump in her throat. She still had not said anything, and she wondered if Olivia thought she had been struck dumb.

Olivia didn't wait for an answer. She swung her leg back to the ground, put both hands into the back pockets of her tight jeans, tilted her head, and grinned again at Ellen. "And then we're having a video party at Heather's. Her mom and dad will be gone and we'll have the place to ourselves. Doesn't that sound great?" Olivia laughed in her shrieky way. "I think if we drop a hint, the guys will crash our party."

The school bell rang then, and Ellen leaped from the swing.

"I don't know," she said finally. "The bell's ringing," she added stupidly.

Olivia bent lazily and picked up her bright blue backpack from where she had tossed it by the swing poles. "So I hear," she said, laughing again and tossing her hair back. "Anyway, you're invited to come," she said. "Tell me your answer later."

Ellen sat in a daze through reading class and math.

She had never in her life bought anything at Richwell's Togs. She couldn't afford it. And a party without a parent there? Her dad was easygoing, but he'd never let her do that. Still, an afternoon with those girls! Ellen imagined herself walking with Abby and Olivia and Heather along the mall stores, laughing and joking. She felt a little chill of excitement at being with both Abby and Olivia at the same time—not on the porch of Abby's house, uninvited, but with them at a mall or at Heather's, part of the group.

Ellen woke up enough to hear Mr. Fitz asking her a question about the Galápagos Islands. "Yes," she said. "The flightless cormorant is an example of an animal adapting to its environment."

Mr. Fitz beamed at her. "Right-o," he said. "Another example from someone else?"

Ellen knew she was safe and sank back into her mind. The biggest question, she thought, isn't whether I could buy something at Richwell's. I suppose I could use my savings.

Jen poked her from behind. "You okay?" she whispered. "You look like you're about to faint."

Ellen turned around to see Jen's grin. She was too stunned to tell Jen what Olivia had said. "Oh, I'm fine," she lied. But she couldn't bring herself to return her friend's smile.

She turned back around and stared out the window at a newly leafed maple tree. And the biggest question isn't even whether I could go to Heather's, she thought. I suppose I could figure out a way if I didn't mind lying.

As Mr. Fitz announced silent reading time, Ellen took out her library book and opened it to words that blurred before her eyes. The biggest question is *why* Olivia asked *me* to go somewhere with the Dandy Dames, she thought. Now *that* really is the craziest thing I've ever heard. Ellen smiled in pleasure and puzzlement at that thought, and opened her science fiction book, *Time Zone, 2053.*

She heard Jen rustling around behind her, sliding folders into her desk, and taking out a library book. Suddenly a thought occurred to Ellen. Jen! None of those other questions are as important as this one. The really big question, Ellen thought, the mega-question, is could I even *think* of going with Olivia if Jen isn't invited?

Ellen heard Jen settling behind her and saw her sneakers stretching out in the aisle. She glanced up at Mr. Fitz, who caught her eye and pointed deliberately at the book he was reading. Ellen began reading.

At first she couldn't get Olivia off her mind. She read fitfully, stopping after every couple of paragraphs to marvel at the invitation. But the pull of the story was irresistible and soon she was deep into her book.

Suddenly Kyle, the boy across the aisle, the kid with the canary-sized brain, tapped her arm hard. He clutched a pink folded paper and whispered noisily in the quiet room, " 'To Ellen,' it says." He held the note high and waved it back and forth.

What a jerk, Ellen thought in panic. She stared at the folded sheet of notepaper waving in front of her eyes, and her breath stopped. She snatched it from Kyle and hid it in her desk.

But too late.

Mr. Fitz cleared his throat and looked sternly at the class. The sound alerted everyone and all eyes looked up. "Ellen Anders," he said slowly and distinctly, "bring me the note at once."

Everyone turned toward Ellen, and she grew hot and red.

She stood slowly, legs weak and wobbly, and walked to the front of the room. "I didn't write it, Mr. Fitz," she whispered. She put the note into his open palm. "I don't know anything about it."

Ellen walked back to her desk and sank into it. Her face and armpits felt drippy with sweat. What could it be? she thought. Who could've written it?

Mr. Fitz opened the note, and the class was silent. He looked at it for a long time. Nobody looked at anyone else. Ellen's heart hammered.

At last he ripped the note into two pieces, placed the two pieces together, and ripped again. He neatly dropped the shreds into the wastebasket. "Olivia," he said, and turned to look directly at her. "If you want to talk to Ellen, please do it in person. Your plans for Pinetown Mall can be made on your own time."

Ellen slumped in her seat, sweating and pale. She felt

twenty-six pairs of eyes turn toward her, and heard everyone laugh.

"Sorry, Mr. Fitz," Olivia said, her voice high and light and full of laughter.

Ellen, face flushed, swung a look around the room, her eyes landing in two places—on Abby's wide-eyed face and on Jen's pinched white one.

11

*E*llen had after-school crossing guard duty, and none of her friends were around when she finally put away her patrol stuff. Avoiding Mr. Fitz, who sat at his desk grading papers, Ellen slipped out the door and trudged down the street. She didn't see anybody on the way home—not her old friends, not the Dandy Dames, not anyone. Her head in a muddle, she barely spoke to Pepper, who crouched, meowing loudly, by the door.

Automatically, Ellen read Dad's note, took the meat loaf from the refrigerator, turned on the oven to 350 degrees, and set the loaf pan on the center shelf. She peeled the potatoes, cut them up, and put them in cold water so they would be ready to cook later when the meat loaf was closer to done. "You're getting to be a pretty good cook," her dad had told her the other night.

At least I can think *something* through clearly, Ellen thought. Even if it's only meat and potatoes. Invitations from Olivia Von Cracken are beyond me.

Then Ellen set the table, scooped some Kal Kan Kitty Stew into Pepper's bowl, and, skipping her afternoon talk show, went directly to her room. She pulled the green diary off the bookshelf, where it now stood among her Nancy Drew and Tolkien books.

After the Abby/Dandy Dames fiasco, Ellen hadn't been able to tell anyone else, not even Jen, about the diary, but for the last couple of weeks she had kept reading her way through it. As she did, she found herself envying her own mother. After all, Kathryn Hoffstrom had a mom, and friends who were not only popular but also faithful, unlike Ellen's own first best friend.

I'll bet those girls—Julie and Carole—those friends of my mother didn't break their pledges, thought Ellen. Katie's problems—a boyfriend who didn't smile at her, baby-sitting for her foster brother, a fight with her sister— weren't problems at all. Well, maybe to Katie Hoffstrom they were.

Ellen held the green book to her chest and flung herself up to her loft bed. She reached down to help Pepper up. As she scratched the cat's neck, she opened the diary to where she had marked her place with an old valentine. It was a passage she'd read before.

Monday, February 7, 1963
Dear Diary,
Tonight I went skating and wow, what a time I had! First I asked my mom if I could put on some lipstick. She said I could. So when I got to the rink, I put some on. My sister Eileen came up later

and asked me about it. I told her that mother said I could. Whew! Freddie was up there and he was real lovey-dovey. He walked Julie and me home. He kept trying to put his arm around me, etc. I would wiggle out every time. He was furious and told me this was my last chance, but that's tough! I think he acts too old for his own good—and for mine! I still like him, though!

Ellen read on to the next entry.

Tuesday, February 8, 1963
Dear Diary,
Hi! It's 10:00 P.M. and I stayed home tonight. Surprise, eh?! This afternoon Julie took a little neighbor girl to the movies and I took the Mattson boys. I guess Mom let me because I was baby-sitting, and the show was only cartoons. Gosh, those kids were hard to handle! The movie was a Bugs Bunny one, and the theater was just plain packed with little kids running around and yelling! We saw Carole downtown, but we could only say hi because we were running to take care of the kids. I think she thought we snubbed her, but gosh, Diary, I was having troubles! You know, I'm pretty sure Freddie was at the youth center with some new girl. Boy, am I burned up! I saw them go in together! Ohhh! I guess he's just dropped me! Oh, well, that's the way life goes! P.S. I don't like it!

Ellen sighed and slipped the red cardboard heart into the book. She lay back, arms above her head and diary resting on her stomach. She thought about Katie Hoffstrom. She sure was a lively kid, Ellen thought, always so happy. Ellen stared up at the ceiling. Katie sure wasn't devastated when her boyfriends dropped her. She just didn't like it.

Maybe Katie Hoffstrom was a Dandy Dame of the 1960s, but there was something about her that Ellen liked—something upbeat. I wonder what she would've done about problems like mine, Ellen thought. Ellen balanced the diary on her forehead and lay very quietly, thinking. Finally, she gave up and plopped the diary onto the sleeping bag. Katie probably would've just had a party, she thought in disgust.

She sat up and swung her legs over the edge of her loft. "A party," Ellen muttered, an idea forming in her mind. "Maybe Jen and I could have a party!"

She thought it over, wondering who might come, and if her dad would let her. Maybe even Abby would come, she thought. And then a really crazy idea surfaced. Maybe Olivia would come. She laughed. Maybe Jen and I could have a party for our whole class. We could invite *everyone,* not just a few people the way Olivia does.

Oh, that'd never work, she thought. Dumb idea. But then she knew what Katie Hoffstrom would say. "It might work! It's worth a try. Go for it, Ellen!"

The chiming of the living-room clock caught Ellen's

attention, and she glanced at the clock on the bedroom wall. She pushed Pepper gently aside and jumped from the loft. Got to get those potatoes going, she thought, and she placed the diary back on the shelf. With a silly little grin on her face, Ellen ran downstairs.

Ellen mashed her boiled potatoes on her plate and spread on some margarine. "So I could do it, Dad?" she asked. "I could have an end-of-the-year party?" She had been talking to her dad about her idea nonstop since he got in the door. "I'm going to see if Jen will do it with me."

Her dad cut off another slice of meat loaf. "Sure, Ellie," he said. "Why not? We've got a big house." He grinned at her across the old oak kitchen table. "It's a great idea. I'm thinking about having a gathering of my own," he said. "An English-department party—a backyard picnic early in June."

Ellen grinned at her dad. "That's a good idea, Dad," she said, and felt happy for him. But she couldn't really take her mind off her own idea. She plopped a glob of ketchup onto her plate and dipped a forkful of meat loaf into it. She ate for a while and then went back to her topic. "But, Dad," she said, "I want to have my whole class. I don't want to leave any kids out."

"That's fine," Dad said. "Kind of an end-of-elementary-school party."

"I haven't had an all-class party since my kindergarten birthday party!" Ellen got up and ran around the table to hug her dad. "Thanks, Dad," she said. "You don't have to help except to be here." She started to clear the table. "You said I was a pretty good cook, remember? Jen is great at baking. Maybe she'll make chocolate chip cookies—or cake—and it'll be a potluck party. Everyone'll bring treats."

She frowned suddenly. "Do you think they'll come?" she asked.

"Well, you won't know till you ask," Dad answered, and he started running hot water in the sink and squirted in some dishwashing soap. He piled the dishes in and started scrubbing and rinsing. "I'm willing to provide the soft drinks in a big tub of ice," he said. "But you have to clean things up before and after your gang is here!"

"Oh, I will," Ellen said.

Dad turned then and looked at her. "Maybe Abby would like to help you and Jen plan the party. I haven't seen your old pal for weeks."

Ellen leaned against the counter, ready to dry the dishes. "I know," she said. "I haven't seen her much, either. She's hanging around more with some other girls." Ellen thought for the millionth time of Olivia's invitation to Pinetown Mall.

Dad scrubbed the glasses and plates, rinsed them, and set them in the dish drainer for Ellie to dry. "Well, friendships change," he said. "But why can't Abby be friends with you and those other girls, too?"

Ellen stacked the clean dishes in the cupboard and

reached for the silverware Dad had just rinsed. "It doesn't work that way, Dad," she said. "We don't all like the same things."

Dad washed the last pots, drained the sink, and wiped off the counter. He rinsed out the dish cloth and wrung it hard, then spread it over the edge of the sink to dry. He put his arm around Ellen's shoulder. "Well, Ellie, before you know it, it may all change again," he said. "And who knows, maybe you'll all like one another." He gave her a hug. "Anyway, the party's a good thought," he said. "It might bring you all together."

Ellen hung the dish towel on the rack. "Thanks, Dad," she said. She felt relieved that she didn't have to explain it all to him. As she began to walk out of the kitchen, she paused and turned back. "Dad," she said. "Don't you think sixth-grade kids are too young to have a party without a parent there?"

Ellen's dad looked at her, his bushy eyebrows raised in curiosity. He shrugged his shoulders. "Well, sure, Ellie," he said. "Yes, I do think so. Does someone want to do that?"

Ellen smiled at him, a wide grin. "Something like that," she said. She picked up Pepper. "I've got a phone call to make," she said, and she took the steps two at a time.

"Ellie," Dad called as she reached the top step. Ellen swung around and looked down at her dad at the bottom of the staircase.

"Yeah, Dad?" she said.

Dad smiled a slow grin and leaned against the door frame. "Guess whose enthusiasm you've inherited?" he said.

Ellen hugged the cat. Her heart beat so hard that it hurt for an instant. "Mom's?" she said, her voice small. When she saw her dad's nod, she said again, "Mom's!" and she danced to the phone in the upstairs hall.

12

*E*llen dialed Jen's familiar number. After a quick hello, she explained about Olivia's invitation.

". . . and after Richwell's Togs, they're going to watch videos at Heather's house and Olivia said that maybe some of the guys would come." Ellen's words ran together as she tried to get them all out at once.

There was a long silence on the other end of the line, and when Jen did speak, her voice sounded weak. "And they asked you to go, El?" she asked. "Both you and Abby are going to be part of that group?"

"Not me," said Ellen. "Abby, maybe, but not me."

"You're *not* going?" Jen asked.

"No," Ellen said. "Of course not. I don't have that kind of money and I can't go to an unchaperoned party. Besides, you and I made plans for a movie on Saturday, remember?"

"Yes, I do remember," Jen answered, her voice quivering. "But I thought 'Olivia-fever' might have made you not remember."

"The movie is at the same mall where they're going," Ellen said. "Maybe we'll see them, and maybe we can talk to them." Ellen fantasized about all of them together—Abby, Jen, Olivia, Heather, herself—looking through the videos in the store, trying to choose.

"But I'd never be friends with Olivia's gang," said Jen.

"That's what I think, too," said Ellen. "But Abby's in that gang now, and she's still Abby."

"I don't think so," said Jen slowly. "She's not *our* Abby anymore."

"That's true," Ellen said. She paused. "But somehow she isn't completely a Dandy Dame, either."

"I want her to be ours," Jen said. "Only ours."

"Me, too," said Ellen. "But I think she's somewhere in between."

"Well, I hate it," Jen said.

"Maybe there's something we can do, Jen," said Ellen. "I have a great idea, and I wonder if you'd help."

"Sure," said Jen. "What's your idea?"

"Listen to this," she said. "I think that you and I should give an end-of-the-year party for our whole class and that we should . . ."

After a long conversation about the party, Ellen climbed at last into her high bunk and tried to let her excited mind relax. The green diary sat on the windowsill where she'd last left it, and she opened it to an entry she hadn't yet read.

"Hi, Katie," she whispered, and began reading.

Friday, March 14, 1963
Grrr, Diary. I'm so mad I could spit. Let me tell you. Today I got into a terrible argument in civics

class and I was so loud that Mr. Lewis sent me out of the room! I'm ashamed of that, but I'm more mad than ashamed. We were talking in class about people emigrating to the U.S. and Joycie Kane, whose dad is a doctor, said that the Polacks should've stayed where they belonged and not come to the U.S. And there sat Marie Krzchinsky, poor old Marie Krzchinsky in her dumb cotton print dress that looks like my mom's housedresses! And Mr. Lewis had just *said* that we *all* were immigrants at one time or another!

Well, Diary, I just blew up and told Joycie that she shouldn't talk that way—and I got louder and louder and all mixed up in my words. And Mr. Lewis said that I was *right,* but that I needed to go out in the hall to cool down. Oh! I'm so embarrassed. What must everybody think of me. What an idiot I am. But it made me so mad!!!

Ellen touched the penciled words on the page, touched the girl in the green book, touched her mother.

"All right, Katie!" she said aloud. "Way to go!" And she closed the diary, tucked it beneath her pillow, and turned out the light.

The next day Ellen entered the classroom with Olivia, explaining that she'd already made plans for Saturday, so she couldn't accept her invitation. Then she took a deep breath. The hubbub of the room covered her voice, so their conversation was private.

"Olivia," she said. "I'm having an end-of-elementary-school party the day after school's out—in two weeks." She smiled a nervous smile. "It's for everyone in the class. Will you come?"

Olivia lifted her chin and looked at Ellen. "Everyone?" she asked. "Boys, too?"

"Everyone will be invited," she said. "Even Mr. Fitz."

Olivia flipped her hair out from her collar. "Well, maybe, Ellen. I'll see," she said. She turned away.

Ellen spoke on impulse. "I'm trying to think of a neat invitation," she said. "If you have an idea, I'd love to see it."

The bell rang, calling the students to their desks and demanding quiet. But during announcements and lunch count, Jen leaned toward Ellen. "We could play Truth or Dare," she whispered. "And Sardines."

Ellen turned around. "And we could rent a scary movie," she said.

"Yeah!" said Jen, her voice louder. "And I'll borrow some good tapes from my brother for the music."

"Okay. Good!" said Ellen. "Do you think anyone'll dance?" The girls giggled softly.

Then Ellen noticed Mr. Fitz going to the Discipline Board, chalk in hand, and she signaled Jen to be quiet.

"Ellen and Jennifer," he said, "you are trying my patience. Here is your warning." He wrote their names on the little rectangle, and the class tittered, surprised that Ellen and Jen were in trouble. The girls blushed and sat straight in their desks.

"Boy, he must be crabby today," Ellen muttered softly after Mr. Fitz returned to his desk.

Kyle heard from across the aisle. "You were just too loud, stupid," he whispered. "What's going on, anyway?"

"You'll see," Ellen said very quietly. "Even you'll be included, birdbrain."

Ellen thought about the party all through math. Maybe we can play charades. Or have a crazy scavenger hunt. She stared at a math problem on probability. Or if it doesn't rain, we could play volleyball. She worked a while on a ratio exercise. Jen can use her brother's great tapes—we can play those during the whole party.

In language class, Mr. Fitz once again had a poetry writing and art session. Kids walked around the room, collecting paper and glue and yarn. Ellen daydreamed about party decorations and couldn't get started on the assignment. She was startled when a sheet of white drawing paper filled with colorful Magic-Marker lettering landed on her desk.

"ONE FOR ALL AND ALL FOR ONE," it said. "COME TO A PARTY AND HAVE SOME FUN!" The blue-and-red bubble letters were filled in with yellow. Green and blue balloons bordered the page, and at the bottom, in fancy calligraphy, it said, "Saturday, June 5—At Ellen Anders's House."

Ellen looked up, startled. Olivia stood at her desk.

"It's an idea for the invite," she said. She had her usual smirky smile on her face, but her eyes looked shiny and excited. Ellen felt relief spread through her body. If Olivia made the invitation, that must mean she's coming to the party, she thought. And if *she's* coming, probably everyone else will, too.

"It's great," Ellen said. She smiled at Olivia, surprised at how comfortable she felt doing so.

"Thanks," Olivia said, and just for a moment, a wide grin covered her face. Then she turned and moved back to her own desk.

The room was in its regular noisy state by now, and Jen risked leaning forward. "What is it?" she asked. Ellen turned around and showed her the paper.

"An idea for the invitation to the party," she said.

Jen's mouth opened, but she was silent. Finally she spoke. "From Olivia?" she said. Both girls closely examined the invitation. "It's pretty nice," Jen said at last. Ellen picked up a red marker and added the words, "Sponsored by Jen and Ellen." Jen smiled.

Kyle reached across the aisle and tried to pick up the invitation. Ellen's hand came down hard and loud on the desk to stop him.

Maybe Mr. Fitz was especially sensitive to their corner of the room because of the earlier ruckus. Or maybe they were being too loud again. At any rate, Mr. Fitz unfolded his long legs and strolled over to Ellen's desk just as Kyle succeeded in grabbing the invitation. "What's this?" he asked. He took the invitation from Kyle's hand and read it through. "Well, it's not a note exactly," he said, and looked at Ellen. "Or is it?"

Ellen's face reddened and she laughed. "Well, Mr.

Fitz, maybe it is," she said. "It should be posted. It's for everyone in the room." She smiled. "Even you, Mr. Fitz."

"Hey, I didn't get to read it yet," said Kyle. He knelt up on his desk and read over Mr. Fitz's shoulder. "All right!" he said. "A party! What time does it start? Will there be food?"

Mr. Fitz carried the invitation to the bulletin board near the door. Several girls gathered around as Mr. Fitz picked up the stapler.

"Of course, Kyle, if there's food you wouldn't miss it," said one girl.

"I'll bring food!" Kyle said.

"Maybe we all can," said another girl.

Mr. Fitz shook his head and shrugged his shoulders. "I don't know about you people," he said as he looked around the room. "I think you're ready to be seventh graders." And he stapled the colorful invitation to the corkboard.

13

When Ellen walked in from her patrol duty post a half hour after school ended, the halls were empty. She hated being assigned to the farthest corner. It meant that she left school last, and alone. She put away her bright orange patrol belt and flag and went into the classroom to pick up her backpack. She paused on her way out the door and read through the invitation. I'll have to write in the time and what everybody should bring, she thought. And the address and phone number. She walked out of the room, waved to Mr. Fitz down the hall, and left the building.

For the first time since Abby was invited to Olivia's party, Ellen felt completely cheerful. She hoisted her backpack over her shoulder and turned toward the sidewalk, humming.

"Hi, Ellen," Abby called from the school-yard swings.

Ellen stopped and turned in surprise.

Abby walked quickly toward Ellen. "Can we walk home together?"

"Uh, sure," Ellen said. Her old anger at Abby flared for a moment, but died as she realized that Abby must have been waiting for her. Maybe she wants to talk about the party, Ellen thought.

The girls walked off the school grounds and down the street toward their block. Ellen felt an old familiar pleasure at walking beside Abby, but she was tongue-tied.

Finally Abby broke the silence. "Are you coming on Saturday to Pinetown Mall and to Heather's?" she asked. "I sure was happy that Olivia asked you."

Ellen hefted her backpack to a more comfortable place on her shoulder. "Oh, Abby, I can't afford to buy clothes at Richwell's Togs," she said. "And my dad would never let me go to a party where there wasn't a mom or dad there. He said so."

"But, Ellen," Abby answered, "you wouldn't have to buy anything big at Richwell's. Just a headband or something." She looked sideways at Ellen. "And her parties aren't wild at all like we used to think. Really, Ellie, all we do is talk and listen to music. Your dad wouldn't care."

The girls turned onto their block, walked a while, and stopped by Abby's house.

"Maybe so," Ellen said. "But, anyway, Jen and I already made plans to go to a movie on Saturday."

"I'll bet Jen wouldn't mind if you went to the movie at a different time," she said. "El, it's neat that Olivia invited you! I'll be there. Please come."

"Abby," said Ellen, "I can't just dump Jen so I can go to the mall with you guys."

"You wouldn't be dumping her," Abby said. She put her hand on Ellen's arm. "Go to the movie on Sunday afternoon with Jen." She paused. "Jen would understand. Besides, maybe we could talk Olivia into inviting Jen some other time." Abby squeezed Ellen's arm. "C'mon, El. Please?"

Ellen turned to Abby and frowned. "I can't do that, Abby," she said. "Jen would be hurt—really hurt." Ellen pulled her arm away from Abby's hand. "She'd get the message."

Abby abruptly started walking up her driveway. "You make me so mad, El," she said. "You won't even *try* to be in with Olivia—even if she asks!"

"Olivia's not a goddess, Abby," said Ellen, her voice angry. "No matter what *you* think!"

Abby looked directly at Ellen. "Well, *you* seemed pretty happy that she helped with *your* party," she said, nearly shouting.

Suddenly Ellen felt the pressure and anger of the last few weeks explode in unwanted tears. "Yes, I wanted her to help!" she yelled. "I want everyone to help." She swiped at her eyes with the sleeve of her jacket. "The party's for our whole class. I want you to help, too." She turned away to hide her crying and started home.

"Ellen," Abby called. "Ellie!"

Ellen stopped and turned. "Oh, Abby, you ruined it," she said, her voice shaky and quieter, her face wet. "The braid, the pledge, all ruined. Everything's different now." Ellen ran then, down the block and onto her porch. She flung her backpack onto the step and landed in the porch swing all in one movement. The words of the pledge ran through her mind.

O blond and black and brown braid,
We promise to be friends, unafraid.

Ellen thought about the braid in its cracker box on the top shelf of her closet and pulled her feet up onto the swing. She wrapped her arms around her legs and put her head on her knees.

Abby *isn't* a friend, unafraid, Ellen thought. She isn't my same friend anymore at all. Ellen thought about the green diary and her mother's friends. Why didn't my mom ever write about fighting with *her* friends? Ellen's mind mixed the braid and Abby and her mom all together, and she let her tears flow. When Pepper leaped up beside her, purring loudly, Ellen put her legs down to hold the cat. She buried her eyes in the cat's fur and cried and rocked until she felt a sense of relief. Hiccuping and streak-faced, she finally relaxed.

Pepper's hungry meows stirred Ellen to action. She picked up her backpack, pulled the mail from the mail slot, and unlocked the front door. She walked through the quiet peace of the empty house to read her dad's note.

Hi, Ellen,
There's nothing much to cook in this house. Want to go out for supper? Check one box. Love, Dad

☐ No, I'd rather eat Cheerios.
☐ Maybe, but only if I can have a brussels-sprout sandwich.
☐ Yes, yes, yes!

Ellen laughed in spite of her anguish. Goofy Dad, she thought, and opened the cupboard for a can of cat food.

"Liver bits, Pepper," she said. "How's that?" Ellen fed the cat and then dragged herself up to her room. She pulled out the diary and climbed into her loft. She opened the window and lay there, diary closed, staring out at the maple tree.

Ellen thought about what Abby had said about Olivia. She's right, I was pleased when Olivia made the invitation. Ellen frowned. And I was also pleased that she invited me to the mall. What's wrong with me, anyway? She sighed and opened the book.

Sunday, April 10, 1963
Happy Easter, Diary! God bless everyone! Hi! This morning my whole family went to Sunday school and church. I dressed all up. I wore my new blouse, new skirt, new shoes, and my new nylon stockings. This afternoon we played baseball and fooled around. Tonight—THE EASTER PRO-GRAM! (Later) Well, it went off all right. In one of the scenes I had to crow like a rooster! Well, thank the Lord everything was okay. I knew my part and

said it fairly well. I crowed okay, too. Bye-bye!
Gotta go to bed.

Ellen grinned at the silly idea of her mother crowing in
an Easter program. She stopped reading when she
heard the creak of her dad's bicycle and his cheerful
whistle.

"Hi, Dad," she called out the open window.

"Hi, Ellie," he called back. "I sure hope you checked
choice number three. I'm starving."

Ellen sat up. "You bet!" she called. "I'll be right
down."

Ellen fiddled with the ketchup bottle as she sat across
the table from her dad at Geraldine's Café.

"I put up the invitation for the party at school today,"
she said. "Well, actually, Mr. Fitz put it up."

"That was nice of him," said Dad.

"Not really," said Ellen. "It was punishment." She
paused while the waiter put down her plate. "At first,
anyway."

Dad picked up his hamburger. "I'm confused," he
said. "Is the invitation posted somewhere or not?"

Ellen laughed and dipped her french fry into a blob
of mayonnaise. "It's up," she said. She ate a while.
"But, Dad," she said.

"Yeah?" Dad spoke through a mouthful.

"Abby and I kind of had a fight."

"I thought you and Abby'd had some kind of dis-agreement earlier this year," Dad said. "Is this a new one?"

"Not really," Ellen said.

"Not really?" Dad said. "Everything is 'not really' tonight."

Ellen shook her head. Dad just can't get it, she thought. She picked up her hamburger and added some ketchup.

"Not really," she said, and took a big bite.

14

The last week of school was busy. The class took tests, cleaned out desks, and cleared bulletin boards. And every night, Ellen and Jen would prepare for the party. On Monday and Tuesday night they baked five batches of chocolate chip cookies and froze them. On Thursday after school Ellen went to the Ben Franklin variety store to buy balloons and crepe paper. As she walked through the colorful aisles collecting her supplies, something familiar caught her attention— some small books on the shelves near the stationery and pens.

These are diaries, she thought, and she picked up a bright red one and looked it over. There was a tiny gold lock attached to a strap that wrapped around the book. A little key hung from the strap. "My Diary," it said in fancy gold lettering on the cover. I need a diary, Ellen thought suddenly and forcefully. I've got to have a diary.

Ellen put the diary back in its place, set her crepe paper and packages of balloons on top of some spiral notebooks, and squatted by the shelf to look at the other diaries. There were some with the days of the week embossed on each page, some called five-year diaries, and some with all the dates written in.

She rummaged further among the books on the shelf, unable to find one she liked. Then she noticed a book with no words on the cover. It had a pastel-colored rainbow on the cover and pinkish white clouds. The background was a pale blue sky. Ellen picked up the book and opened it. Blank pages stared at her. Lovely blank, lined pages. Ellen stared back at them for a long time.

Then finally she smiled and carefully put all the other diaries back into their neat piles. She counted her money, tucked the rainbow book under her arm, picked up her crepe paper and balloons, and headed for the checkout counter.

That evening Jen and Ellen strung crepe paper streamers around Ellen's house and set out blue and red and yellow balloons to blow up just before the party. The house looked festive and nearly perfect when Jen got her things ready to go home. Ellen picked up the variety-store bag, empty now except for the rainbow book.

"Jen," she said, and looked at her friend. "I'm going to start writing a diary." She took the book out of the bag and put it on the table. "This is going to be my diary."

Jen looked at her and then down at the book. She picked it up and opened it slowly, her gentle smile turning into an enthusiastic grin.

"That's a neat idea, Ellie," she said. "This is a pretty

book." She studied the rainbow. "Maybe I'll do one, too. Summer'd be a good time to start."

Ellen smiled back and the girls said their good-byes.

After Jen had left, Ellen put the rainbow book on her shelf next to her mother's diary and climbed into her loft, forgetting her nightly ritual with Katie Hoffstrom. She fell asleep wondering when she should start writing in her diary.

The next day was Friday, the last day of school. When Ellen walked in that morning, the only thing still displayed in the empty classroom was the party invitation. The room was echoey and lonely-looking, but nobody seemed to care. It was as though they had already given up ownership of the room to next year's group of kids. Everybody yammered on and on about summer vacation, about going to junior high school in the fall, and about Ellen's party.

"I can't wait for tomorrow," Kyle called to Ellen. He sounded excited. "I'm bringing caramel corn. Home-made!"

"You going to the party?" kids called to each other.

"You coming, Mr. Fitz?" someone asked.

"I'll be there," said Mr. Fitz, a wide grin on his face. "I wouldn't miss it!"

Olivia stopped at Ellen's desk on her way to stacking up her textbooks. "I suppose your dad'll be there," she said. "Abby tells me that you have to have a chaperone."

Ellen pulled her head out from inside her desk where she was doing a final scrubbing with a soapy sponge.

"Um, yes," she said. "He will be."

"That's silly," said Olivia, rolling her eyes.

Ellen held the wet sponge and didn't answer.

"But I'll be there, anyway," Olivia said. "I'm bringing avocado dip and corn chips."

Olivia stacked some books on the shelf below the windows and walked back past Ellen's desk.

"Olivia," Ellen said.

Olivia stopped again. "Yes?" she said, eyebrows raised.

"Is Abby coming, do you know?" Ellen said.

Olivia tossed her hair back. "Well, how should I know?" she said. "Ask her yourself."

But Ellen didn't. She couldn't.

After school Jen and Ellen ran to Ellen's house and, after feeding Pepper, began making the three cakes. They stirred and baked and frosted and decorated. Using chocolate sprinkles, they lettered the cakes. "CONGRATULATIONS!" said the first cake. "GOOD," said the second. And "LUCK," said the third.

Ellen's dad came home in time to admire their work and lick the bowl.

They put the cakes on the big dining room table and covered them with plastic wrap. Then the girls cleaned up the kitchen and Jen got ready to leave. "I'll be over early," she said. "I'm so excited."

"Me, too," said Ellen. She picked up Pepper and the girls stood quietly looking around, admiring the party-ready room. The doorbell startled them.

"I'll get it," Ellen's dad said. He came out of the TV room, walked to the front door, and opened it. "Well, greetings, stranger," he said, voice loud and hearty. "Come on in."

Ellen and Jen looked at each other.

"Hi, Mr. Anders," said a familiar voice, and into the living room walked Abby. She carried a thick folded white packet.

"Hi, Ellie," she said. "Hi, Jen." She looked around at the room. "It looks nice," she said.

Ellen nodded. Nobody else spoke.

Abby handed the packet to Ellen. "I made a banner," she said. "I—I stayed after school and asked Mr. Fitz if I could make a banner on the computer, and he said yes and so I did," she said, all in a rush. "It's for the party."

Ellen began unfolding the long sign. Her dad reached out to hold one end and Ellen walked across the room, unfolding as she went.

Jen read the words aloud as they became visible. "MR. FITZ'S . . ."

"GANG," Jen read as Ellen opened another segment.

"NUMBER," Jen said next.

Ellen took two more steps and the banner fully unfurled.

"ONE!" Jen finished.

Little computer-generated hearts surrounded the words. The lettering was in blue and red and yellow. Jen went and held Ellen's end, so Ellen could walk out into the middle of the room to see the whole sign. She read it, "Mr. Fitz's Gang—Number One!" and sighed. She turned to her former best friend. "Thanks, Abby," she said. "It looks great."

"You're welcome," Abby said. She stood quietly, unsmiling. Then she turned quickly toward the door. "See you tomorrow," she said and let herself out the front door.

Jen left a few minutes later.

"We'll put the banner up tomorrow," Dad said, and he folded it. "That was nice of Abby."

Ellen sighed again. "You're right, Dad. Friendships do change," she said. She hugged him good night and went upstairs.

Ellen put on the old T-shirt she used for pajamas, brushed her teeth, and washed her face. She turned out all but the bed lamp and climbed into her loft, her mom's diary in hand. Pepper leaped up, too. The banner is nice, she thought. But Abby and I'll never be "friends unafraid" again. She leaned back against her pillow and stared up at the ceiling. Maybe just regular friends, though, she thought. She pressed her fingers along the binding of the old green diary. And maybe I'll even be friends with Olivia if she can ever quit acting like queen of the universe.

Ellen snuggled under her covers and opened the diary. I'm glad Jen's my friend, she thought as she settled in to read a new entry in her mother's diary.

Saturday, May 5, 1963

Dear Diary,

Hi!! Ya know what? WE GOT TELEVISION!!!! It's a 17-inch table model on a swivel stand. It only cost $85. Isn't that a marvel?!? We keep it upstairs because we don't have an antenna yet and Dad says we have to keep it upstairs till we get one in about two weeks. It has rabbit ears and the picture comes in real good, even without an antenna. I'm going to stay home tonight and watch it. None of the kids know we've got it yet. Golly, are they going to be surprised when I tell them!

Ellen reached down to set the book on the table. She turned out the light, rolled next to the open window, and looked out at the stars. Oh, dear, dear Katie Hoffstrom, she thought. She cuddled under the quilt and hugged Pepper. "If you were here, Katie, I'd want you at our party, too," Ellen whispered to the stars. Then she closed her eyes.

TOWN OF ORANGE
PUBLIC LIBRARY
ORANGE, CONN.